So this is love

LOLLIPOP AND OTHER STORIES

Gilbert Reid

KEY PORTER BOOKS

Library and Archives Canada Cataloguing in Publication

Reid, Gilbert
    So this is love : lollipop and other stories / Gilbert Reid.

ISBN 1-55263-636-4

    I. Title.

PS8635.E398S6 2004   C813'.6   C2004-903534-7

ONTARIO ARTS COUNCIL
CONSEIL DES ARTS DE L'ONTARIO

The Canada Council | Le Conseil des Arts
for the Arts | du Canada
since 1957 | depuis 1957

The publisher gratefully acknowledges the support of the Canada Council for the Arts and the Ontario Arts Council for its publishing program. We acknowledge the support of the Government of Ontario through the Ontario Media Development Corporation's Ontario Book Initiative.

We acknowledge the financial support of the Government of Canada through the Book Publishing Industry Development Program (BPIDP) for our publishing activities.

Key Porter Books Limited
70 The Esplanade
Toronto, Ontario
Canada M5E 1R2

www.keyporter.com

Text design: Peter Maher
Electronic formatting: Jean Lightfoot Peters
Printed and bound in Canada

04 05 06 07 08 5 4 3 2 1

For Dianne

Contents

Pavilion 24

MAYBE IT WAS THE DELIRIUM, but he remembered it this way.

They had no room and no supplies, so they put the wounded and dying where they could. He was set down on a mattress and a pile of burlap on the floor in Pavilion 24. This was three hours after they'd amputated his right leg just above the knee without anaesthetic and without antiseptics.

He lay on the mattress not able to think for a long time, only dimly aware that fine snow was drifting through the holes where the high slanted roof had been shattered by random mortar fire.

The second day he felt more clear-headed and the pain was worse.

The third day the pain had dulled a little and he felt twitchings and aches in the ghostly foot. He wondered if they'd eaten his leg. He'd heard that people were eating human flesh, though he didn't want to believe it. Strangely, the idea gave him pleasure. Perhaps his leg would have made a good stew or broth.

On the fourth day the doctor brought a young woman. Her head had been shaved and her skull was tied tight in white bandages. She was maybe eighteen or twenty, and he could see she was very good-looking, even with the shaved head and bandages. She was badly bruised but handsome, with big grey eyes, strong arched eyebrows, a generous mouth. She could walk, though she was very weak and the doctor held her by the elbow and guided her down onto the mattress next to his. The young woman sat on the edge of the mattress, six inches away, and then swivelled around, lay back, closed her eyes, and put the back of her right hand over her face. Yes, she was a very good-looking young woman, certainly considered beautiful in ordinary circumstances. He wondered if he would ever feel desire again.

The young woman was wearing soft leather boots that must have cost five hundred dollars, faded blue jeans, a black turtleneck sweater, and a brown leather jacket. It was the sort of jacket Jimmy Stewart wore when he played a pilot in one of those World War Two movies. She must have been rich, the young woman, rich and fashionable, probably a student from one of the bourgeois families.

"She's a Serb," said the doctor, looking at him.

"Ah," he said softly, looking at the doctor, then at the girl.

The doctor went away.

For a while he just lay and stared at the roof, at the way the light straddled in sideways and struck the high cross-timbers, at the slanted, broken tiles of the roof itself. It was warm-looking light, though the air was very cold. Before the war, this had been a storage shed used for tractors, for tools, greasy machinery, bags of grain, not for humans.

He looked at the girl. She lay still, the hand over her eyes, its fingers curled. A bloodstain had appeared on the bandages.

He looked away. He wondered why the doctor had told him she was a Serb. Involuntarily his hand went down to where he kept his pistol, packed in the burlap at the edge of the mattress. The metal grip felt cold under his fingers. He was beginning to discover sensations again: the touch of his fingers on metal, the smell of snow in the air, sensations that were slowly fighting their way back through the throbbing frontier of pain. Maybe the doctor wanted him to kill the girl. Yes, that was it. Doctors were not supposed to kill their patients. But a wounded, mutilated militiaman, yes, he could do it. No questions would be asked. Not many anyway. He thought he would do it simply—it came to him very clearly—just shoot her.

Bang!

The Serbs had come to his village—really a middle-class suburb—when he had gone to get the car. It was a small raiding party, but they had guns and nobody else did. They went from house to house. They were drunk but methodical. They raped his wife, his two daughters, and his eight-year-old son. Then they shot them all, mutilated the bodies, and departed. When he got back, nothing remained of his family but the bodies. And the writing in large letters in blood on the kitchen wall that told him exactly what the Serbs had done. Just in case he didn't understand.

Since then he had killed Serbs. It was the only meaning he could give to his life.

Until he was too close to a mortar shell when it landed. His fingers tightened on the pistol.

The young woman moved. He turned to look at her. Her hand no longer covered her eyes. She had big grey eyes, intelligent-looking eyes, but there was something strange about them. Maybe it was the pain.

"I'm blind," she said.

"Blind?"

"The head wound...The optic nerve centre... Something was severed...They explained. But I'm not sure."

"You're a Serb."

"Yes." She turned her face away. "I heard him tell you."

"Yes." The ghostly leg throbbed. A mortar was firing somewhere; there were distant explosions, probably in the suburbs on the far side of the river. The old man at the end of the pavilion was sobbing.

"Are you really blind?" He shifted to make the pain easier, but made it worse.

"Yes," she said. "Maybe it won't last." Her face was inches away. Big grey eyes, bruises, a few cuts.

He pulled out the valuable box of wooden matches. She winced slightly when she heard him strike the match against the side of the box. He held the flame close, in front of her eyes, moved it back and forth—no contraction of the pupil, nothing at all, just big immobile grey eyes staring at him.

She blinked. "Satisfied?"

"I guess so." He put the matchbox back under the mattress.

"What happened to you?" The eyes were still staring at him.

"A mortar. Lost my right leg. Above the knee."

"I'm sorry."

"Thanks." He paused. "I'm sorry about your eyes."

"It may get better." She was very young.

"The doctor couldn't say. He's..."

"He's a Muslim. You're a Serb."

"Yes."

He thought for a minute. "I don't think he would do that." He wondered if he would have done that, if he'd had the chance. Would he have blinded the girl? A slip of the scalpel? An extra incision? No, he wouldn't have done it, he wouldn't have blinded her; that was the sort of thing a Serb would do. But he would have killed her, let her die, let her rot. He turned away, so he didn't have to look at her eyes.

"No, you're right. He wouldn't have done that," she said. Her eyes were staring at the ceiling.

The moonlight lit up snowflakes drifting in under the shattered rafters. It was bitter cold. The pain in his leg was clearly defined now, cutting like a knife, up his thigh, snaking into his belly, into his testicles, and clear up to his shoulders, branching like a tree.

He wanted to shout, to cry, to scream, but he knew it would do no good. He wanted to stuff his mouth with burlap and sob, but he had a clear sense of himself, of his dignity. He held himself in stiff silence. If only he could have a drink of water!

"It's bad tonight, isn't it?" She spoke in a whisper.

"What do you mean — bad?" His voice was thick with pain.

"The cold. The pain."

"Does it hurt?" He tried to turn to her and grimaced. The blood had welded his amputated stump to the mattress.

"No. Your pain. I meant your pain."

He didn't say anything.

"I can feel it from here. You're trying to hold it in."

He didn't say anything.

"Do you want a glass of water?"

He sighed. He waited. The pavilion was silent. No one had come for hours and hours. Where were the doctors? Where were the nurses? Finally, he said, "Yes." He hesitated. "How are you going to get the water?"

"You guide me."

So she stood up, finding her balance, and he told her to walk straight ahead to the opposite side of the pavilion, to touch the wall with her left hand, to walk along the wall, to turn the corner, then to stop, then to bend down and touch the bucket, to grope for the faucet with her fingers.

"I've got it," she said.

"Turn it," he said.

"I know how to turn a faucet," she said.

He heard the gush of water but could not see it.

"It's freezing," she said. Her voice carried the strange resonance of invisibility, making the empty spaces of the pavilion seem tactile, audible. He was the one who was blind, he thought. He blinked upwards. Snow was still drifting through the holes in the roof, but it melted and disappeared before it reached the debris-cluttered floor.

The water stopped gushing. The silence suddenly seemed very large.

"Here I come," she said. "Watch for me." Her voice was hollow, echoing from around the corner.

He twisted his head to watch her. She was a shadow, but he could see her clearly. Her right arm was outstretched and her fingers were touching the wall, while the fingers of her left hand were curled around the bucket handle. She looked like a dancer or an acrobat. Her jeans were so tight her legs looked like they were encased in dancer's tights, and the jacket, with its collar turned up, made her shadow look like that of an Elizabethan courtier. Shafts of moonlight struck the rough stuccoed wall—in the blue metallic light snowflakes slowly drifted.

"Stop after a couple of steps," he said. His voice sounded like a stranger's: a man talking to a blind woman he didn't know and whom he intended to kill, maybe tonight, maybe tomorrow, maybe later. His leg started to throb. God, it was cold!

"Here?" Still touching the wall, she had stopped.

"Yes." He winced. "Turn to your right."

"Three o'clock," she said.

"Three o'clock?"

"A quarter turn to the right. That's the way they talk to blind people."

One foot at a time she turned, until her back was to the wall.

"I see." He winced. He would have to cut himself loose from the mattress.

He saw her press her shoulders to the wall to make sure of her bearings. She was not stupid, this young Serb, not a peasant barbarian like so many of them.

"About five steps," he said. "Straight ahead."

She advanced carefully.

"Stop. Put down the bucket."

"There!" She put down the pail and then edged forward until she could feel the mattress. She sat down, grasped for the pail, and slowly, very carefully, pulled it towards her.

"You learn fast," he said.

"I was scared."

"I have a glass," he said.

"The water's freezing," she said.

He handed her the glass. She turned it in her hands, dipped it into the water, and reached out, giving him the first drink.

Later the water in the bucket developed a crust of ice. She had moved her mattress against his. She was sleeping, beside him. For a long time he lay awake. Her breath and his breath were both visible in the frosty air. He felt her warmth through the jeans and the jacket. He had pulled some burlap over them both. Animal heat was the only heat they had. Her breathing was even and slow. His leg throbbed. "How can she sleep?" he wondered. Perhaps she was not suffering pain; perhaps she had brain damage and that made her sleepy—though she was certainly not confused when she was awake. Of course, she was young. Well, it was a mystery.

Here he was, a Muslim, condemned to be her enemy. Her people had killed everything he loved, and he wanted to kill her—why? Revenge? Some abstract sense of justice? What?

She stirred, turned on her side. Her arm went up over his shoulder, behind his neck. It felt warm. She was still asleep, her breathing unchanged. Gently, he moved some of the burlap and left her arm where it was, her smooth skin warm against the nape of his neck.

"So what happened to you?"

"I was hit on the head." She didn't say anything for a long time. He could see her breath.

Somewhere there was a burst of machine-gun fire. Somewhere an old woman stopped screaming.

"Don't want to talk about it?"

"No. No, it's not that. I mean, I don't want to talk about it. But it's not that. I'm... They were Muslim—Muslim, like you. I was at my grandmother's..."

A burst of mortar fire. Not too far away. Dust and flakes of paint fell from one of the walls.

"Where are we now?" she said. She reached her hand out in front of her face, brought it back, touched the tip of her nose, her forehead, her lips.

"Nowhere."

"Nowhere," she said. "Yes, that's where we are." She shifted so she could face him. She smiled. She had a beautiful smile, made even more intense by the empty, wide-eyed stare. "You want to kill me, don't you?" she said. "You've been thinking about it. You were thinking about it when I was bringing the water. Arrogant Serbian bitch, you were thinking. I'm right."

"You're clairvoyant."

"I thought so." The smile was far away now, frozen like the blind eyes.

"But maybe I can't."

"Ah."

"No one has come."

"Yes. It's strange."

"It's as if we've been forgotten."

"Yes."

"We're alone. I can't move. Not yet. So I need you."

"I can't see. So I need you." She smiled again and sat up. She fumbled for the bucket, broke the ice crust with a quick rap of her knuckles, and scooped up a glass of water. She held it out to him. He took it. "I think this is very funny and maybe somebody is laughing somewhere," she said.

He gave her the glass. "Thank you," he said.

"There were five men." Her eyes were staring straight ahead, at the wall opposite, or at some place in empty space. Snowflakes drifted down from far above. The sunlight was blue like summer dust. "Five men. One of the men was crying. His family had been killed — his whole family. I knew that. He was a lawyer. I had met him. I knew his son. His son was dead, and his wife, and his other children, five children. I knew it already, but he told me. He told me again. He wanted to be sure I knew.

"We were the only Serb family. There was no danger. They could take their time. They beat Grandmother and raped her. And then they shot her. They'd tied me to the kitchen table. Me, they wanted to keep to the last. That's what they said. His friends said he could have me to himself. I would be his..." She shrugged.

"Revenge."

"Revenge. Yes, revenge. I suppose. You know, she was sixty-eight years old. A retired schoolteacher. She had lots of Muslim friends."

"We all had lots of friends."

"Yes."

"What are friends? What is love?"

"Yes." She turned to him. The blind eyes caught reflected sunlight. "What is anything?" She shrugged again. "Anyway, they left us alone, him and me, in the kitchen. He untied me, spit in my face, slapped me, tore off my clothes. He tried to rape me. But... But then..."

"But…?"

"He couldn't."

"Couldn't?"

"No. He was crying. He couldn't. So he zipped himself up and pushed me back on the table and put the barrel of the gun up inside me and it tore me and I thought now he is going to pull the trigger and kill me and I said, 'Please don't do it, you don't want to do this,' and I told him I was sorry about his family but that I had nothing to do with it, and I had been a friend of his son, we'd studied math together, I'd even been to their house. 'You don't want to do this,' I said. I tried to be very calm. I was surprised at myself. I felt sorry for him. He was looking at me and tears were coming down his face. He took the gun out of me and started to hit me on the head with it. From side to side. Like he was slapping me. I shielded my face, but he hit my head again and again. Then he stopped. I couldn't move. The butt of the pistol was covered in blood, bits of hair. I was conscious, I could still see, but I couldn't move. He fired the pistol three times. Close to my face. He looked at me and nodded. Like we would meet again. Then he walked out of the room."

"And they didn't come back."

"No."

"But you're blind."

"Yes. It happened later. I got up. I went to my room. I got dressed. Then I started seeing double. I was bleeding too much. I couldn't stand up. Then I was blind. I went out into the street. Someone took me. Someone helped me. A Muslim, I think."

That night she had a fever. She lay close to him and she was sweating heavily. The head bandages suppurated a black, sweet-smelling liquid. Why had no one come to change the bandages? He shouted. But nothing happened. No one answered. He'd feared infection; he'd feared it more than anything else. There were no antibiotics, so once an infection started you were... Well, you were almost certainly dead.

She shivered; sweat poured off her. She was like a furnace. He held her close. Through layers of burlap and their clothes—her jeans, sweater, jacket, his military pants, underwear, oiled-wool mariner's sweater (a gift from his wife during a holiday in Italy)—he felt her heat. He wiped the sweat from her forehead. She shivered and nodded her thanks, bit her lip, shivered again. "I'm going to die," she whispered.

"No."

"It doesn't matter." She shivered. Her arm was under his neck, her heat entering him like love. "I'm sorry," she said, "I'm sorry for what happened to your family. For what happened to you."

"Sorry? I thought you Serbs were all paranoiac: everybody's guilty but me."

"Not all of us." She paused. "Not me. Not now."

He felt her forehead. She moved. For a moment her lips touched the palm of his hand.

Later she fell into a deep sleep.

He lay watching the moonlight. It made strange designs on the broken beams, the shattered wall.

He reached down and took the pistol, the warm, smooth metal, the well-used grip. Smooth metal is so simple, so simple. It's a solution to everything.

He put his arm around the girl and held her. She murmured, stirred, bit her lip. Her teeth gleamed, but she didn't wake. Her cheek was next to his, her breath mingled with his. He wondered if she would ever wake. He wondered if he would ever wake. It was a nightmare, an unending nightmare.

Fresh snow dusted the frozen ground. The sunlight was almost too bright. Both men blinked.

"And what's in there?" The young United Nations officer had a clipboard. He was trying to be helpful, trying to be thorough, poor fellow. But it was useless and there was nothing more to be done.

"There?" Dr. Nadal squinted and pointed at Pavilion 24.

"Yes. There." The United Nations officer squinted from behind his clipboard. He was tired and frustrated. It was an impossible mission. Look and report, but don't do anything. Don't give them supplies. And don't offend anybody. Neutral, neutral, neutral. Dr. Nadal and his staff had no supplies, no equipment, and yet...well, they did work miracles. But not even miracles, in this godforsaken country...

"There's nothing in there," said Dr. Nadal. "Pavilion 24—that's where we put the dead. A natural freezer."

"I see," said the officer. He made a check on his clipboard.

"Well, I guess that's that," said Dr. Nadal.

"Yes," said the officer. "That's that."

Dr. Nadal accompanied him to the UN jeep.

He watched the jeep disappear: an inspection, a friendly couple of words, but no supplies, no help, no hope. Dr. Nadal was tired, so tired he was indifferent to the cold, indifferent to the searing light, indifferent to the mortars and snipers, to the fact that, smeared with blood, he looked more like a butcher than a doctor. Indifferent. There was, he knew, no hope. No hope at all. Not from anywhere. Not from anybody. "Yes," he said, "that's that."

Soon We Will
Be Blind

SOON IT WILL BE DARK.

Soon we will be blind.

He is talking; I listen. His voice is like rough-edged country music, melodic and sad. I love him. He knows I love him. And so it is that love can go unsaid, with all the other things we will never say.

"Now, you won't remember this, I guess, 'cause you were just... Hmm, how old you were? Maybe five, six? In there somewhere. So you won't remember..."

I love him, but, in my mind, I object: who is he to tell me what I can or can't remember? Why, hell, I remember lots of things. I say: "I was nine."

"Nine?"

"Uh-huh."

"Nine?"

"Yep."

"I can't believe it. Nine!"

"Well I was nine. That's what I was." As I say this, I close my eyes and remember. Let's see, the first thing, yeah, the first thing I remember, it was one of those sunny days. Little fluffy white clouds floated up high in the big blue over the wheat fields. They always gave me a funny feeling in my tummy, those little fluffy clouds. Like they were going somewhere, somewhere I'd never be able to go, discovering mysteries and adventures I would never know.

"Yeah," I say. "It was early summer."

"That's right. Summer. Early summer." He holds a long silence after that. He's good at silences, at those long, old-fashioned silences people don't know how to hold any more, when you just listen to the silence and to the sounds that come along casually, like gifts, maybe the fluttering of a bird, or the barking of a dog—or somebody shouting for somebody else in the evening quiet, far away. Listen long enough and the sounds are like music. Beautiful and melodic and meaning nothing, if you know what I mean.

Love, maybe, is like silence.

You don't have to talk.

Things it takes a long time to learn.

"That's right. Summer," he repeats. "The girl turned up on a summer day. She was older than you. Maybe ten, maybe eleven, I guess, but I don't suppose it made much difference to her."

"No," I say. Though that's not true. It did make a difference to her. Everything made a difference to her: she saw and understood everything. But I say "no" just the same.

Time passes.

Slowly I let the silence wash over me.

"You want another beer?" I say.

He looks at me as if I'd woken him up. He stares at the

glass in his hand at the end of his straight, tanned arm, nods, and shoots me one of those abashed quick smiles I used to love so much and still do love with a warmth and excitement that almost frightens me. The light is dying quick. Soon I won't be able to see him at all.

"Yep," he says. "I'd like that."

I unfold myself up out of the deck chair and go into the house to get the beer out of the fridge. Beer ice-cold and straight out of the bottle, which is the way he likes it.

I like fetching things for him. I like the feel of his eyes on me. I like anticipating what he'll want, what he'll need, what'll bring a quick, shy smile to his face. And I like moving from the dusky cool of the porch inside, into the empty rooms where, in stagnant grey pools, the heat of day lingers.

As the fridge door opens, cool air and light come out, and chill white mist. I reach in for the beer.

I close the fridge door. It clicks heavily and I see stars. I blink away the bright after-image and hold the cold bottle in my hand.

I stand for a minute and listen. There is not a single light on in the house, and I suddenly know this is a moment, I guess one of those moments, that I will hold in my head and my heart and turn around and around and look at for years, and remember, maybe forever.

I take the beer out to the man. I hand it to him. He grunts an affectionate thanks. I lower myself down and stretch out my legs. I turn my feet this way and that. I like the look of my ankles. Now I can just see them in the dark.

Soon we will be well-nigh invisible: ankles and eyes and legs and all.

But now I let my heart quiet down. I want to listen. I want to be still.

Quiet, my heart: Let's listen.

"Like I said, you probably don't remember..." His voice comes out of the dark; it startles me.

"I remember lots of things."

"You do, eh?"

"I remember being up at night in my bed and listening to you and Mom talking at night. Out here, on the veranda. You guys sat in your rocking chairs in the dark. All the lights were off. Just the night coming in. Just like now. And you'd talk. Maybe you'd say something. Then there'd be silence. Then maybe ten minutes or so later she'd say something. Then another ten minutes and maybe you'd say something. I couldn't hear your words, just the sounds of your voices. Sort of like music. Soft music."

"You remember that, huh?"

I can tell by his voice he's comforted now with his beer in his hand and us sitting here—just us two—sitting here in the dark. He finds it difficult to look at me—to look me in the eye and know that I am his. He sometimes looks at me sideways when he thinks I'm not looking: I feel it on my skin and how it lingers afterward in his eyes. At one time it used to frighten me, but I don't mind it any more, nor judge it at all since I too take pleasure in similar equivocal moments. In the thickening shadows, we are almost blind, almost at peace.

"She came on a summer day," he says. I hear him tilt up the bottle.

"Yes."

"A day in summer. Say, June."

"July, later maybe. Maybe August. It could have been August." I shift uncomfortably. Doubts multiply. I'm beginning to feel things. I'm beginning to remember. "No, it was June. Jake hadn't left yet. And then all the things that happened that summer...She was there for all of them."

"May, June...August...September," he says. He falls silent. We sit together and let the sounds of the night wash over us. Somewhere a dog barks, a hollow, lonely sound.

He clears his throat.

"She was wearing a little white thing," he says.

"A cotton dress."

"A cotton dress."

A white cotton dress with a couple of seams and pleats and some bleached-out flowers for decoration was all she was wearing, and, underneath, bleached panties with holes in them. All freshly washed and pressed. Somebody'd tried to look after her real good. Somebody poor. The old leather and buckles on her shoes had been carefully polished. Those were the days when simple things were real things. You wanted them to last. You took care of them.

"That little cotton dress was about all she had." He sips at his beer.

I can't see him at all now. Just feel him, in the dark,

close to me, stretched out in his chair, his long legs straight out in front of him.

"Uh-huh."

"You were out in front."

"Uh-huh." I sip at my beer. "In the hammock."

"Ah, the hammock! You remember the hammock!"

Oh, yes, I remembered the hammock. It was a canvas hammock, with faded white and green stripes. It hung between two big old gnarled and knobby oak trees next to our driveway, and the earth beneath the hammock was beaten bare and hard and black from us kids swinging in it like crazy and falling out and rolling on the ground and tussling—with hammerlocks and bearhugs and squirmings and wigglings and laughing like crazy—to see who would get in the hammock and who would have to push it so it swung higher and higher and higher. Drunk with flying so high. Lying in that hammock you could look up into the branches and leaves. If you twisted way back, the world flipped upside down: suddenly the fluffy clouds moved lazily, dizzily, on the blue floor of the sky, the trees and the house and the fields hung into nothing, like so many cow's teats. Any minute, you thought, they're all gonna fall off.

And I remember the girl—the girl she was then—standing suddenly in the driveway as if she had come from nowhere, as if she had been planted there, standing stiff and solemn in that white, neatly pressed cotton dress on the dusty gravel driveway. In that instant I knew she had been put on the earth just for me.

I stopped swinging in the hammock, slowly righted myself, and almost managed to fall on my head. But instead I flipped myself neatly over and landed on my two bare feet and walked straight down the driveway without a pause.

She was more beautiful than any child I had ever seen.

"Hello," I said.

She didn't say anything.

"Who are you?" I said.

She didn't say anything.

I was about to get annoyed and scream and holler, "Maaaaa!" when she reached into her one pocket on the front of her dress and pulled out a little card and handed it to me. "My name is Annie," in block letters it said.

"Annie?" I said. I looked up at her.

She bit her lip and nodded. Her eyes were watching me carefully. Her hair was jet black and cut in bangs that went straight across her forehead. Her skin was chalk white, her eyes coal black, and her lips were bright like lipstick. I noticed her eyebrows and eyelashes, each one of them so neat, it seemed like somebody had painted them on.

"You can't talk or something?"

She looked at me for just an instant, as if she were figuring out a puzzle. Then she bit her lip again and nodded. She smiled.

"Maaaaa!" I hollered.

"She and you got on like a house on fire, which was something I was grateful for. Mysterious, though I guess it was natural, she being so beautiful and gentle and all, before it happened. And I guess she sort of worshipped you." He stretches, I can hear his jeans as he uncrosses his legs.

"She's still beautiful."

"You've seen her?"

"Yep." Nine months and four days ago. It's marked on the calendar: a freezing November day, galoshes and scarves and overcoats, and sleet on the windowpanes, clogging the windshield wipers. Heater won't start. I'd gone to the library to look up some technical information on a water-soluble poisonous chemical for a libel case involving a newsmagazine. I'm defending the good guys, as usual. So, there I am, down in the stacks, mousing around, dreaming of a hot coffee and bagel or croissant, and I turn a corner and...and this young woman, sliding a big book back into place, turns toward me, it seems, in slow motion: profile turning slowly, face appearing, and suddenly her smile is almost too big to believe.

"I've often wondered," he says, "about how all that happened. We know some of it, but not all. Not by a long shot. Like, why she was left in front of our house."

The night is thick. No stars, no moon, no lights visible except, far away, a light in one of the farmhouses.

"Maaaa!" I bawled. Tactless of me I guess, but I'd discovered something new and interesting—a little girl standing in the middle of our driveway who couldn't speak. "Maaaaa!"

Annie stepped back, alarmed. Her dark eyes were wide open. Consternation, I would have called what was on her face, if I'd known the word.

"Come on," I said. Startled by her fear, I reached out my hand.

She looked at me carefully, reading my lips I guess, and took my hand.

"She's deaf and dumb, the poor child," said my mother. She was wiping her hands on her red and white apron while leaning back against the sink the way she sometimes did. She pushed back a strand of hair and crossed her arms.

The county police had come and a doctor who had a farm on the other side of town. Everybody stood around talking. Dr. Goldstein poked at Annie for a long time. He spoke to her carefully, slowly enunciating each word. She nodded. She knew what he was talking about. But she wouldn't tell anybody where she came from or who she was. When they asked, she crinkled up her face like she was going to cry, so they gave up and all agreed they would find out sooner or later. But they didn't, not for a long time.

Mom pushed herself away from the sink and poured more milk into our glasses. Annie looked up and nodded her head with a little jerk, which I guess was her way of saying thanks.

I thought this was interesting, so I picked up the plate of oatmeal cookies and offered her one, just to see if I'd be honoured with the same intense stare and little jerk of the head.

She took a cookie, looked at me, bit her lip, and made the very slightest nod.

So I grinned and gave her a little nod back, at which she

smiled. So I guess I was rewarded sort of double for understanding that I was just a kid, not an adult, and that she was not a toy.

"Rain," he says.

And there it comes: big drops streaming down, a quickening patter on leaves and grasses, just beyond the veranda, just beyond our outstretched feet.

"Want to go in?"

"No." I shift my legs. I'm very comfortable, I like it here. "I like to listen to the rain."

"Me too."

"Rain, rain, go away...remember?"

"I remember."

The rain patters on the veranda roof, on the railing, on the edge of the floorboards.

It's hard to explain the thrill I feel when I am quiet with him, or when we do something physical together, when our actions interlock like the pieces of a puzzle. When I was a kid, I used to help him wash the car, or do carpentry in the workshop, and if I handed him tools when he was working on the engine or building something out back, I felt I was somebody, really somebody.

It reminds me of harvest time. In those days, men came to help with the harvest, a whole team of men, and I took out lemonade to them in the fields, hauling it in coolers on my little wagon. The men were big and often wearing just shorts, and they were tanned and golden and seemed like gods to me. They all thanked me and gathered around and I could smell their sweat and clean men's smell and the straw and hay and I was the centre of attention and very happy.

Things come flooding back. I remember.

The summer Annie was with us she came out to the fields too. We both served the iced tea and lemonade. I think she liked it as much as I did. She was flushed and happy and kept wiping the sweat from her brow and smiling and ladling out the drinks and looking carefully into the men's faces to be sure she understood what they wanted.

There were paths to take and narrow dry rutted roads to follow to get to the fields. It made it difficult to manoeuvre the cart, so Annie and I had to work carefully to avoid upsetting the coolers. I pulled the cart and she walked beside it, keeping her hands on top of the two top-heavy coolers. But each time we made it intact, and the men came towards us, all golden, and all of them were smiling.

Among the golden young men that summer there was one in particular who was very handsome, or so I remember him. He came from England or New Zealand. I forget which. He was called Jake and he spoke with an accent. He was very young, I suppose, maybe eighteen or nineteen, which was young in those days, with blue eyes and thick blond hair and clear skin tanned very dark, and he wore loose cut-off blue jeans and mostly went barefoot. He had nowhere to go, so he slept out in the barn.

One night he chased Annie and me around the garden. We were weaving in and out of the bushes, and when he caught us he tickled us and that was the first time I heard Annie's voice.

It was laughter, a pure high child's laughter, bubbling over.

When he finished tickling us we lay on our backs on the grass, all three of us, and looked up at the sky where the first stars were coming out. Already the dew had made the grass damp with the cool of the evening.

Then he sat up, cross-legged, and told us the names of some of the stars. He was careful so Annie could see his face. There was just enough light to make out the movements of his lips. I could see Annie was concentrating hard. He told us about Venus and about the Big Dipper and the Little Dipper and the North Star, which told you where the north was.

While he was telling us the story I saw that a man had been watching us. He was standing in the driveway close to the hammock, holding a pitchfork and smoking a cigarette. Much later I thought that probably he'd been standing there all the time, watching us run and joke and be tickled and struggle and laugh, and that maybe that was when it all started.

His cigarette glowed red in the dusk and gave me an eerie feeling, so I concentrated on the stars and put my arm around Annie's shoulder, and we both looked up.

"See the big W? That's called Cassiopeia."

Jake made a half-globe with his outstretched fingers and rotated his hand to show us how the night sky seems to swing around because it's really the earth that's going around.

While we're looking at the stars, I think about the man with the cigarette. He is a big man and has no hair on his head, which is shaped like an egg. He works for my dad and lives in one of the farmhouses and has a wife that looks almost exactly like him—two big pale closed pudding faces with tiny pale watery blue eyes that squint at you. He's an itinerant worker, Dad says, from somewhere in Eastern Europe, the Ukraine maybe, maybe Russia. He doesn't talk much, but I had already noticed how he watches me when I play in the barn or in the barnyard. He smiles sometimes to be friendly I guess, but it's a funny smile because his eyes are so small and bright and he's missing some teeth, and the smile stays on his face too long. So I just make a quick smile back and get on with my playing. "He and his wife seem to have no friends," Mom says. "She's a strange woman, never comes out, never talks to anybody. I wonder about them."

"He works hard," Dad says. "He keeps to himself. They've had a hard life, they have nowhere to go."

"Still," Mom says, "they give me a funny feeling."

It's like ping-pong. I look back and forth as they discuss. So does Annie.

"So the moon goes around the earth," Jake is saying, doing a diagram with his fingers. "Do you ladies understand?"

Annie nods and looks at me.

"Uh-huh," I say. "We understand."

"And the planets move around the sun. I think that one right there"—he points up into the sky—"might just be Jupiter. Let's see..."

We are both cradled against Jake and looking up at the sky, following his pointed arm.

I steal a glance towards the driveway. The man and the cigarette are gone. I suddenly wonder if I ever saw him at all and feel even spookier.

"Yes, ladies, I think that might very well be Jupiter."

Jake left us a couple of weeks later, back to university in England. During harvest time he had been part of the family, Mom's favourite of the young and golden men. Often he ate with us in the dining room, which was for special occasions and special people only. It occurred to me for the first time then that maybe Mom and Dad wanted a son but got me instead. It gave me a funny feeling—just for a second I felt I'd ceased to exist.

Jake liked us a lot—Annie and me—because we were excited and excitable, just on the edge of becoming women, and he was old enough not to worry that we were still children.

"I'm in love with you both, you know that, ladies."

"Jake! Don't say that!"

"Head over heels. I swear!"

"That's yucky, Jake!"

"Yucky or not, ladies, it's true romance and true love. Just like in books."

That last night Mom organized a party and Jake made a speech that ended with a little bow. "To your health, ladies," he said, and we emptied our glasses. It was okay, because it was apple juice.

But soon the more serious thing happened.

It is a frosty evening in late fall, a smell of winter already in the air. The sun is gone but at the edge of the sky it has left a deep red streak. Then it turns pale green-yellow, and then, higher up, a dark hard black, with ribbed clouds radiating out, full of ripples of broken red.

The stables are a warm place in the chilly dusk. It is milking time and the first time I'd taken Annie.

I show her everything.

"Be very, very careful," I tell her. We walk among the cows, the big heavy dusty sides of the cows heaving close to us, and the chalky-muddy smell of their black-and-white hides tickling our noses. The smell of piss and wet cow flap mixed with straw is like an envelope around us.

"The milking is all automatic, see."

We crouch by one of the machines. The cow is chewing. It turns its head and its big eyes look at us. There is a plaque above her stall. "This cow is a champion cow," I say. "She gives more milk than any other cow."

After a while we wander apart, inspecting different cows and some calves in the pens.

I lose track of Annie. I start looking for her and go towards the dairy. Then I hear a noise. It's a pail turning over. I push open the door and go into the dairy, which is a very clean space separate from the stables. I'm about to shout, "Annie!" but then I remember it's no use shouting, not for Annie.

I come into the chalk-white room and at first I don't know what I'm seeing: Mr. Kalscheck in his boots and his pitchfork dirty with manure leaning against the wall.

"Mr. Kalscheck," I say. "Hey, Mr. Kalscheck!"

He's leaning over Annie and she's fighting him. I can't see her clearly, but I can see her arms flailing, and her legs are kicking and her skirt is down. At first I think maybe she's done something wrong, but Annie never does anything wrong; she's so careful, so gentle.

"Hey, Mr. Kalscheck!"

His pants are loose. I come up and pull at his pants. "Mr. Kalscheck!" I pull at his pants again. He swings around and hits me—bang!—right across the face.

"I don' wanna hurt her," he says. His face is all sweaty and his eyes look smaller and funnier than ever.

Annie's face is terrified.

Mr. Kalscheck grabs me and hits me again. Behind him Annie stumbles back and falls down. She pulls up her panties and her skirt—both are torn. Her mouth is open like a black hole, like she wants to scream but no sound comes out. Mr. Kalscheck turns back to Annie. He reaches out for her. She shrinks back.

In my mouth I taste blood like when I have a nosebleed, warm and salty.

"Mr. Kalscheck! Leave her alone!" I shout. He spins around and grabs me by the collar and holds me up so my feet are kicking in the air. "Mr. Kalscheck, I'll tell Daddy!"

Mr. Kalscheck starts shaking me so my teeth are rattling and then he rips my shirt and pants right down the middle and grabs my underpants and rips them too. "Stop!" I try to kick him. "Stop!" I try to say, but my teeth are rattling too much.

He pushes me against the pasteurizing machine, and I fall down. Annie is standing up now and Mr. Kalscheck is standing over me. His pants are open and his thing is sticking out and I look at it and think something horrible is going to happen to me but I don't know what. I feel sick and my stomach spins down I don't know where into some dizzy black place inside.

Mr. Kalscheck grabs me and pulls me up and presses me against him and presses his thing between my legs and it's hard and big and hurts and his fingers are trying to get between my legs too, and I kick.

Over his shoulder I see Annie. Her eyes are very big.

"Help! Annie!" I shout. Annie looks around.

"Stop! Stop! Stop!" I scream. His fingers are hurting me.

Annie grabs a milk pail and climbs on the coolers. She smashes the pail against Mr. Kalscheck's head, *wham!* and then again, *wham!* and the pail bounces out of her hand. She jumps on his back, scrabbling, clawing.

Mr. Kalscheck swings around and hits her hard and she bounces back across the dairy like she'd been shot out of a gun.

Mr. Kalscheck goes after her.

I pull up my pants and remember seeing his pitchfork leaning against the wall.

I run to the pitchfork, grab it and point it at Mr. Kalscheck. "Mr. Kalscheck!" I shout, and he turns away from Annie and comes at me and I level the pitchfork at him and the end of the handle gets stuck against the big heavy coolers, wedged there, I try to get it unstuck, I can't move it, I want to hit Mr. Kalscheck with the pitchfork but I can't move it, and he runs straight at me, straight belly-first into the prongs of the pitchfork, and the pitchfork doesn't budge because it's wedged solid, and it goes straight into him.

Mr. Kalscheck stops like he's surprised and he looks down. His hands are waving around like he's trying to swim. He backs up, taking the pitchfork with him. I let go.

I am nine, I think.

I am nine and something is happening.

Annie has her fist in her mouth and is chewing on it.

Mr. Kalscheck backs up some more, dragging the pitchfork with him. He looks down.

"Mr. Kalscheck?"

Mr. Kalscheck pulls the pitchfork out of his stomach and looks down. The pitchfork is red.

Mr. Kalscheck drops the pitchfork and sits down on the floor. His face is all sweaty and looks funny.

Annie still has her fist in her mouth.

"Mr. Kalscheck?"

Mr. Kalscheck's shirt is all red from the belly down, a dark, dirty red. And his pants too and his thing, which is all curled up.

I go to Annie. She takes her fist out of her mouth and looks at me and shakes her head. I don't know what she means but I take her hand and we both look at Mr. Kalscheck.

"Mr. Kalscheck?"

"Uhhhh!"

"He's hurt."

Annie nods. She's solemn now, very calm. Her dress is all torn and dirty. Mr. Kalscheck looks up at us. He tries to say something but he can't say anything.

"Mr. Kalscheck?"

His eyes are clouding over, but he nods.

"Mr. Kalscheck, I'll get Daddy."

Mr. Kalscheck nods and leans back and lies on the floor. His big stomach is covered with blood and there is blood on the whitewashed floor, spreading out.

"It was a tragedy, any way you look at it."

"For me, it was Annie's going away that was the worst."

"For your mother too. She loved Annie."

"I know."

Dad knelt over him. "Kalscheck, what the hell did you do? What the hell did you do? I've got a mind to kill you, you know that, Mr. Kalscheck?"

Mr. Kalscheck whispered something.

Dad listened. His ear was close to Mr. Kalscheck's mouth. Dad listened but he didn't say anything; he just put his hand on Mr. Kalscheck's forehead and he held his wrist. Then we heard the siren of the police cars and ambulance.

Dad's jeans were red with blood when he stood up.

"What did he whisper to you, Dad?"

"Who?" He's startled out of his silence, and I realize how far my own memories have carried me. I drink some more beer. "Who whispered?"

"Mr. Kalscheck. When he whispered to you."

"Oh, oh, that! I didn't know whether to laugh or cry. At first I didn't think I'd heard him right. You remember that, huh? Well, that's the moment I really wanted to kill him. And it was the same moment when I felt...I hate to say it, but I felt sorry for him. I felt...I guess pity is the word for what I felt. A terrible thing..."

"What did he say?"

"He said, 'I never had no children...never had...,' then he sort of faded out."

"'Never had no children'?"

"Uh-huh."

"That's what he said?"

"That's what I think he said. Yes, that's what he said."

"No doubt about it." Dr. Goldstein was kneeling in front of us. Our panties were down around our ankles. His glasses were very thick. "He tried. He certainly tried. Scratches. Abrasions. Some bruising. No penetration though. They were lucky."

We looked down at ourselves.

Dr. Goldstein stood up. "You were very lucky young ladies," he said. He put his hand on Annie's shoulder.

"Brave young ladies," my mom said.

We pulled up our panties.

"Yes, that's right, brave young ladies."

"Time for a hot bath, then, you brave ladies," my mom said.

I don't know when it happened, but Annie and I are sitting in the back of the car, and Dad and Dr. Goldstein are in front, talking. It is night and the car is parked somewhere back near the barns and stables.

"So, what are you going to do?"

"I don't know."

"It could have been serious."

"I know, I know."

I can hear them and I am very interested because I know they are talking about Mr. Kalscheck. Annie can't hear them because she can't see their faces. She put her arm around me and her hand pats my hair. I snuggle close. Annie always smells very nice.

"What about Mrs. Kalscheck?"

"No place to go."

"Hmmm."

"They don't have anybody."

"If you don't press charges, nothing happened."

"I know."

"It's a big responsibility."

"I know."

"He might do it again."

"He's old."

"Doesn't mean that he won't try."

"He might. Everything's a big responsibility. If there's a trial, the girls will have to testify. Do you know what that will do to them? And a deaf-mute girl nobody knows, beautiful like she is! Just think of it! Newspapers. Photographers."

Dr. Goldstein sighed. "Maybe you're right." He looked back at us. "How are you girls doing?"

"We're happy. We're warm," I said brightly.

Dad pursued his thought. "Mrs. Kalscheck can stay until Kalscheck gets out of hospital. Then they pack and go."

"So nothing happened." Dr. Goldstein turned away.

"Nothing happened."

Mom said that Mr. Kalscheck should be put away in a box and never let out, but Dad said, "What about Mrs. Kalscheck?" and Mom said, "To hell with Mrs. Kalscheck." I opened my eyes wide and looked at Annie and she looked at me.

It was after Mr. Kalscheck that Annie was taken away from us. Her mother had been found in a hospital down in the States beaten up by the man who was supposed to be Annie's father. Her nose was broken and one arm and several ribs and she'd been in a coma for a long time. Annie was taken to the States and put in a special school.

Later that fall I got a postcard from Jake, who was in Cambridge, England. Sitting at the kitchen table, in my squiggly writing and concentrating a lot, I wrote him a letter telling him that Annie was gone and that Mr. Kalscheck had gone crazy and Annie'd hit him over the head with a pail and I'd stuck him in the belly with a pitchfork. Jake wrote back and told me not to forget him or Annie. He'd never forget us. We were two real ladies and true cowboys, pail- and pitchfork-wielders, he said. When he got his degree he was going to New Zealand to farm, he said. Cambridge was too misty and humid to see the stars, he said. "The English are not a sublime people, because they can't see the stars," he wrote, so I guess he was from New Zealand after all.

I asked Mom what "sublime" was.

"It's when you feel you're very small, and everything is very big," she said.

I went out to play, and thought about that. It was dusk and already dark and the ground was frozen and there was a fine dust of snow on the black earth and on green grass, which was crisp under my boots. I looked at the lighted window where Mom was preparing dinner like she was framed in a warm yellow picture and she looked up, squinted, and waved at where she thought I might be. I looked at the sky. It was an empty cold dark blue, and the fields were dark and flat and bare. The trees looked spindly and funny. Far away the woods made a low, ragged black line against the sky. I ran back into the house where my mom was and where the lights were always on and there were oatmeal cookies in a jar on a shelf and bottles of milk in the refrigerator. But now that Annie was gone the house seemed empty.

Annie wrote me a long letter in her neat writing and told me what she was doing. She asked me if we could be friends forever. She missed me and Mom and Dad and Jake. I wrote back saying we were friends forever and ever, and blood brothers, and not to forget it

Then we lost each other as people do, drifting apart, each going a separate way.

Inexplicably I suddenly became a very ambitious and serious pupil. My room was unnaturally tidy; I spent long hours on homework, even on weekends.

"Whatever happened to you?" Mom said. "Sure you don't want to go out to play? Do you want an oatmeal cookie?" she said.

From Annie I got a postcard now and again, and photographs over the years of a very beautiful young woman, same jet-black hair, same stunning eyes and brilliant colouring. Sometimes I stuck the photos above my desk. I'd look at them, late at night, dreaming I don't know what, and then I'd stick my nose back into my books.

Voices in the night:

"I worry about her."

"She's all right."

"She's so serious. She hasn't got any friends."

"She's becoming a woman. That's difficult. You should know."

"I know, I know."

"She'll find her way."

"She's so...detached. I think I've lost her."

"It's growing up," Dad said. "We all lose everybody, in the end."

"Smell that?"

"What?"

"The flowers. Lilacs, roses..."

"Yes."

"The rain brings it out."

"It's beautiful, Dad."

"Your mother loved those flowers."

"Yes."

"I've planted the new beds of roses. Where she wanted them. And the lilacs. Along the left fence. You can almost see them. In the moonlight."

"Yes." I pause, and then I say, "I think I'll go up now." I kneel and pick up the tray and put the beer bottles on it.

"Don't bother, honey, I'll do it."

"No bother."

"You leave those things. I'll just sit here."

"You sure? It's damp now."

"Hasn't hurt me yet. I like the quiet."

"Night." I lean and touch him on the shoulder and kiss his forehead and his hand touches my hand briefly but I know he is far away, in another time, with another love.

In the upstairs hall I turn on the light and look at photographs of them when they were young, Dad and Mom: brave, naive, looking startled to be together. They are a very young couple, not knowing what the future will hold. No idea. How much courage it must have taken! To start it all, the farm, the business, the two of them, the struggles and uncertainties: two startled young faces staring at an invisible photographer.

The next night he drives me to the airport. We eat in the airport restaurant and watch the planes come and go.

Then we are suddenly at the departures gate, suddenly dry-eyed, suddenly two strangers.

"Nice you came."

He looks smaller in the airport.

"I'll come back soon."

"I'm counting on it."

We embrace and then, gently, I pull away from him.

"I'll call tomorrow, Dad."

"I'll be there." He shrugs and smiles, the sheepish smile, and I feel a rush of love, of loss.

As the plane rises and arcs around I look down on the patterns of light and darkness and try to guess which of the lights might be his car heading back north or where in the darkness of the country the farm and the old house might be. Then we are over lakes and forests and then over nothing, and I pick up a magazine and flip through it, and finally take a newspaper and read it carefully because for the last four days I have not followed what has been happening in the world at all.

It is almost midnight when the taxi leaves me in front of the house, a townhouse in a row of fine restored brick townhouses. All the windows are dark.

I let myself in.

Without turning on any lights I walk up the stairs and through to the bedroom. A bedside reading lamp is on. She is lying on the bed, in her simple black nightgown, half-twisted out of the covers, a book open in one hand. Her eyes are closed and her face is turned sideways.

Gently I put down my things and kneel by the bed. I touch her hair, rearrange one strand that has fallen across her eyes. Her eyes flutter open. She rubs her nose with her knuckles, reaches out, touches my face and smiles.

"Hello, Annie," I whisper.

I am home.

After the Rain

WE ARE OUT ON A BALCONY. This is Paris and it is spring, quite a few years ago now.

"Looks like rain."

"Rain? Did you say rain?" I reach out my hand.

"Yes, rain." Robyn lays her hand on mine. "Soon it will rain."

Below us there is a large garden. It is enclosed by thick, high walls of stone. During the day, nuns, dressed in black, walk up and down. But now it is night and the garden is empty and dark. Only the gravel pathways show—ghostly white in the dark lawns and bushes.

"You're not happy." Robyn's fingers are on my wrist.

"Sure I'm happy."

"No, you're not."

"Oh? How do you know?"

"I know." She releases me, turns away.

"It's *me* we're talking about."

"I know."

"It's *my* feelings. So if I say I'm feeling—"

"You're fooling yourself."

"How can you know what I don't know about what I

feel? I mean, I'm me, right? So I should know what I feel and what I don't feel."

"Of course you are you, darling." Robyn looks at me, smiling now. The rain has begun to fall. It gives her a halo, a misty halo of light. "It's just that sometimes things bother you. Things you're not even aware of. Things you don't want to think of. Things from the past."

"The past?"

"Well, things happen. Things change."

"*Our* past?" Our past was a taboo subject. By keeping silent about our past, we could remain friends.

"Our past." Robyn is looking at me intently now.

"Well, our past would of course make me suffer."

"Oh, you sleaze! You're not going to pretend, at this late date, that you're full of regrets, are you? That you're a romantic? You're not a romantic, not really."

"You don't think so?" I swallow the rest of my drink. It's raining harder. We really should go in, I think.

"No, I don't think so, darling. But I love you, I really do. You are such a good friend."

Out on the balcony, in the dark, our glasses were now empty. The air was wet. Robyn ran her fingers through her wet hair. Her hair was short and black. It glistened. The lights were glowing on the Eiffel Tower. Mist like rain—or perhaps it *was* rain—passed in front of the peaked dome of the Sacré-Coeur on Montmartre. It looked like a sea squall passing in front of a ghostly volcanic island.

Robyn and I went back in to the party and, like the old lovers we were, we separated, searching out other conversations, other stories.

Time passed...

I was pretty drunk already. It had been a long party. Robyn was on the other side of the room, deep in conversation with Roger. What they had to talk about I couldn't imagine. I'd been talking with a French girl who was a Marxist, but I kept noticing another small girl. She had copper-brown hair, gold-brown skin, and dark eyes brightly flecked with mica. It was as if she were made of burnished gold. I thought she must be part Polynesian—one of those beautiful half-breeds the French Empire threw up and then left behind. It was a hot night. The girl's hair was damp. It hung in limp, ragged strands like ropes over her shoulders, down her back.

She was talking to a tall, impatient man, an intellectual of very decided opinions who didn't like to listen to anybody else's thoughts on anything. Her head tilted to one side. She listened to him, nodding.

Out of the corner of my eye I followed her every gesture. She had a small body—neat, muscular, sensual—and shapely, tanned legs. She was swaying back and forth in her thin tunic like an impatient kid.

Followed by the Marxist, I went over, introduced myself. The Marxist understood. She gave me a glance and towed the tall bore away towards the bar.

The golden girl and I talked.

The situation was very promising. Something, I felt, would happen. She was clearly lonely. "That man was dreadful," she said. "So many ideas and not one of them right."

Later, still later:

Robyn is looking at me across her drink. "Cooler outside, darling," she says. The rain had not stayed. It was just a shower, but it seemed to have cleared the air.

"Do you mind that I still call you darling, darling?" Robyn fills my glass.

"I like it."

"It's rather old-fashioned."

"It's pretentious."

"I like that too. It's you."

"My, aren't we cruel," I say. I watch as she fills her own glass and puts down the bottle.

Again we go out on the balcony. We look down on the slanted tin rooftops, the chestnut and plane trees. Not too far away is the Eiffel Tower, all lit up, and a glimpse of the Seine. Far below, a *bateau mouche*, lit up like a store window, passes under a bridge. I lean against the balcony balustrade. "That girl. Do you think I can go to bed with her?"

"Fuck her, you mean?"

"Yes. I guess I do mean that."

"Try. She's an adult."

"You don't mind?"

"I'm not her mother. I'm not even her sister. Maybe you'll be good for her."

"Maybe."

"Maybe? So why do you want to fuck her?"

"She's fragile."

"I see. So you think you are going to save her. You think it's a therapeutic fuck. Save the Waif. Or do you want her to be fragile so it'll be easier to hurt her?"

"No. I don't want to hurt her."

"Don't hurt her."

"I won't."

The light of the Eiffel Tower is reflected on Robyn's face. A big elevator, a cube of tiny lights, crawls slowly up one of the tower's legs. "I don't want to stop you having fun with her, if that's what it will be — fun."

"I —"

"You men always have to prove yourselves, don't you?"

"I guess we do."

"It's like a bloody scoreboard. If you can't fight a war, you have to fight us. You notch us up — so many cunts conquered, notch, notch, notch — so many notches like slits on the old rifle stock." She laughs a bitter little laugh. "Like bull's-eyes in darts. A chat among the lads over beers. *Oi, you got a bull's-eye there. I'll stand you for an extra pint, me lad! Oi!* You are children, really. Children."

"Don't be bitter."

"I'm not bitter. I'm amused. We had a good time."

"Yes."

"You're like a brother to me now."

"Oh?"

"A brother I'd like to fuck." She puts her hand on my arm. "When you've finished with her, fuck me. But not tonight."

"You're sure?"

"*Auld lang syne.*"

"Let's go out."

We left the party, took the elevator down and went out the front door. It was eleven P.M.

The sidewalks were glowing and there were halos around the street lamps. We found our usual café almost empty. Robyn ordered oysters.

"So do you think I should...go with the girl?"

"You don't have to do anything to please me, you know."

"No."

"Or avoid doing anything."

"No?"

"No. I'm satisfied. I'm sated with life, with love, with you."

"I see."

"No. Maybe you don't see. I like being with you, talking, just talking—just drinking and talking and eating oysters. It's like we're very old and very wise, and we've seen and done all there is to see and do and we know all there is to know. And now we can afford to love with ease, mutely, blindly, without thinking."

I thought about that. I could wear slippers. The dog

could bring me the morning paper rolled up in his mouth.

The storm broke. In rattling waves, rain lashed against the plate glass of the café, the awnings flapped wildly. The waiter came, clasped his hands in front of his tuxedo and asked if we were happy. We said we were happy but that we'd be happier if we had another bottle of the same. Robyn gave him a special smile and asked for another plate of oysters. The waiter nodded, smiled, went away. He seemed very pleased. Robyn's charm is invincible. I have never seen it fail.

Tonight, she wanted to drink white wine, eat oysters, carefully sliding them out of their shells and into her mouth, and to talk about talk, about listening, about not listening, about women, about men, about men who don't listen — me, for instance. I never listen, she tells me, and when I listen I don't understand, not much anyway.

"Remember that time you didn't listen?"

"I had indigestion."

"Yes. And that other time."

"I was exhausted. I had an early flight."

"Tonight you will listen, won't you, darling?"

"Yes."

"Don't worry. The waif will be waiting for you when you get back."

"I guess."

"She's lonely, you know. She's afraid." Robyn looked at me over an oyster; Robyn has the most expressive eyes.

"Afraid?"

"Yes, afraid." She looked away, towards the street. My glance followed hers.

The rain hammered against the glass. The light changed; a bus went past; a man in a flapping tan raincoat ran for it.

"Is it so old-fashioned to love, darling?"

"Love?"

"To yearn? To feel in your bones you cannot live without that very special person?" Robyn lifted her glass. "Love. The spice and meaning of life."

"Love is difficult to discuss. To talk about."

"Yes, you men hate to talk of love."

"Yes."

"You don't even like to talk about sex. Not really. Real sex is too messy, too real for you men."

"Really?"

"You are all cowards." Robyn refilled our glasses.

"We're too scrupulous," I said. "We don't like to get caught out in a lie. Let's talk about love. If you say 'I love you,' it implies all sorts of things. It's like a contract. We men don't like to break contracts. We take words seriously. Words are pledges; love is serious. It's easier to talk about something else."

"Sometimes you talk the worst rubbish, you know."

"I do my best. When I'm with you I do my best. So no love talk. Not between us."

"I know. Nowadays people just talk of fucking. I do myself. *How many fucks did you have today, luv? Is that particular cunt good pussy, a good fuck? Cushy pussy? Is he a good fuck?*

A real stallion? A real stud? I once posed for some beaver shots. Did you know that?"

"No."

"Well, I did. I was behind in my rent."

"The flat in rue Grenetta?"

"Yes."

"Did you like it?"

"What a bloody stupid question. Just like you, darling, to ask a girl a bloody stupid question. Well, it was a cold bloody studio with the wind whistling all over the place and rain like sleet outside—last December, miserable, just before Christmas—and I'm stark naked lying on a table with my legs wide open and they spray oil on it so you look all wet. Dripping with excitement, you know."

"Pretty picture."

"It was. Like a bloody gynecological examination. Why men want to stare at pussy on paper, I'll never fathom."

"Well it's...cathartic, perhaps."

She laughed. "Perhaps?"

"Yes."

"You are funny! They put drops of yogurt too."

"Yogurt?"

"To look like sperm, you idiot."

"Ah."

"They wanted it to look like some fellow had just squirted all over me. Couldn't hold it in. Charming idea, I thought. I got the photographer chap to give me three hundred francs extra for the yogurt. It wasn't in the agreement."

"So your legal training came in handy."

"Always does, darling." She slid in another oyster.

Robyn is a lawyer, quite a successful one. But in those days she was penniless, struggling to finish a postgraduate degree in international law. Sometimes she fell behind in her rent. Sometimes she moved suddenly, finding a new flat, camping, shacking up, doing whatever she needed to do.

She reminds me how one summer night she had stayed out all night with nowhere to go. "Walked my bloody feet off." She laughs. "Luckily, it was a warm night. You were somewhere else—London or Rome, I don't know—and I didn't have the keys to your flat. So I just walked. The city was empty, pretty much empty. Paris is so beautiful when it's empty. A chap came along and said, I see you are walking. Yes, I'm walking, I said. Mind if I walk with you, he said. You're not some bloody rapist, I hope, I said. No, he said, I'm quite harmless really, just lonely, he said. Well, come along, walk, I said, but it'll be a long night, I said. I don't mind, he said. We walked till almost dawn, then we had coffee and croissants at the Gare du Nord and he took a train to Berlin. I saw him off. I waved. He waved back out the open window. He kept waving until the train disappeared. He was a German, studying philosophy, he told me, in Heidelberg. He looked like one of those Nazis in the movies, you know, the ones who are so blond and so handsome you positively know they are evil. Never saw him again." Thoughtfully Robyn tilts an oyster, squinting at the traces of sand in the shell.

The rain had stopped by the time we went back. The plane trees dripped big fat slow noisy drops. There were new flat green leaves on the sidewalk and on the asphalt. Tires hissed. Everything smelled of spring and ozone. The air was clean; the world was new. The neon signs and traffic lights were vivid. Tomorrow, we agreed, would be a beautiful day.

"It's good to be alive."

"Yes."

"Perhaps we could have a life together someday. Do you think?" Robyn narrowed her eyes, glanced sideways.

"Perhaps."

She laughed and took my arm. "Oh, but the man is cautious! A man's word is a man's pledge!"

At Robyn's door, we kissed on the lips. Her lips tasted of wine. I guess mine did too. "Good night," she said and closed the door. She opened it again, a crack. "I love you," she said. "Don't hurt her." Her face disappeared. The door was shut.

You are the one I should be fucking, I thought. You are the one I should hurt, you are the one I should say all those lying words to. You are just too beautiful and vulnerable and maybe after all I do love only you.

I walked back to the apartment building, climbed up to the last landing, got out the key, pushed it into the lock, turned it and eased the door open. The apartment smelled of spilt wine and roast lamb. It was dark except for one candle on the dining-room table. The girl was sitting alone at the table, half a bottle of rosé in front of her. Her tunic was off one shoulder and her skin glistened gold and wet in the candlelight. The heavy dampness from before the storm lingered in the apartment.

"*Tout le monde dort*," she said.

"Yes."

"I didn't think you'd come back."

"We just went for a drink and some food. Robyn was still hungry. She wanted oysters." I took off my jacket and put it on the back of a chair. "Three dozen oysters."

"I like Robyn."

"She likes you. She feels protective."

"Does she?

"Yes. She's a woman's woman. A man's woman too, really." I thought about what I was saying—yes, it was true. Robyn was both of those things.

"I have ice cubes. Do you want some wine?" Her hand slid out to the bottle.

"Thanks. Yes." I sat on the chair next to her and put my hand on her bare shoulder. It was warm and smooth and oiled by the dampness. She glanced at me as she handed me the glass. "It's not very good wine." Her glance was not unfriendly; it had the blank innocence of a child's first glance at a stranger. "Everybody's gone to bed. I was just sitting here thinking. Roger's with Julie. Pierre-Henri is with Margot. Marie-Aude and Sylvie went home. And you and Robyn went out."

"I see."

That was that brief period in western civilization when everybody went to bed with everybody else. If you didn't go to bed with somebody, you went out.

She held the glass against her chin. "I was beginning to feel sorry for myself. So I drank. I don't usually drink."

"I see." My thumb and fingers explored her collarbone, the tendons of her neck.

"I am far away from home. Very far away."

"Yes."

"I am of mixed blood. That does not make it easy. If I were not drunk I would not be saying this to you. It is not something I talk about, my mixed blood. Nobody talks about it—not when I am there, at any rate. I think we all think about it, all the time or sometimes, I don't know."

"It's not important."

"Yes, it is important. It is and it isn't important. It isn't important for you. You are whole."

"I'm not sure about that. What do you mean by whole?"

"Not wounded. You are simple. Not split. You cannot imagine what other people are."

I slid the other shoulder of her tunic free. The candle flickered golden on her skin. Through the window, I could see the glow of Paris in the rainy sky.

"Robyn loves you, I think." She refilled my glass; both her shoulders were naked now, gleaming flickering gold.

"Do you think we can find a bedroom?" I put my hand around her neck.

"I think so," she said. "You're the one who lives here, aren't you?"

"I think so."

"You think so."

She had a hard, wiry, smooth body, like an electric eel, all slippery muscle, writhing, struggling, and wrestling in a quick sheen of sweat.

I had a headache, but swam up to the surface.

Outside, the sky was a mottled grey-rose.

She rode me; I traced her ribs with my fingers.

She made hungry love. That I remember. A fragile vessel she was. All gold and brown and smooth.

A small medallion on a silver chain spun between her breasts.

She was crying.

"What's this?" My hands held her wrists, my fingers and palms felt a rough edge, a ripple, crossing both wrists.

"*Moi*," she said. "*C'est moi.*"

Her face nuzzling into my face, her cheeks wet with tears.

Two scars, serious scars, on both wrists, the type of scar a sharp knife or an old-fashioned horn-handled straight razor can make. She must have tried, tried very hard. *This is me. Oh, yes, this is me—a scar, two scars. But you cannot understand, you are whole.*

Don't hurt her.

I made love more seriously, even ferociously: I used her,

I suppose. I was violent. I used my man's strength—the scars, the vulnerability, were exciting. *Those who suffer, you can hurt them, you can love them, they must love you back, they cannot deny you—the maimed, the crippled, the blind.*

She began to cry.

"Don't cry."

She cried harder.

"Don't cry. Please don't cry."

"It is not important. You think I am a whore."

"No. No, I don't."

"It is not important. Maybe I am a whore."

"You are not a whore."

"It is not important what people think." She dried her eyes and fell asleep, one arm across my chest. Her body, small breasts, rib cage, and hips were against my side. One thin leg over my leg.

I lay looking at the reflections of Paris on the ceiling. The door to the balcony was open and the lace drifted in— a breeze, after the rain, a cool breeze.

When I woke up she was gone, and there was a note on the chair with my trousers. I blinked at it, holding it in my hand, rubbing my head. "Thanks. You were still asleep." The handwriting was very careful, even elegant. I folded the note and put it in my pants pocket.

Robyn was sitting at our usual café table reading the morning papers. She looked up from *Le Figaro* and pushed her big tinted glasses up over her forehead. "Well?"

"Yes. I did."

"You old bugger."

"If I were a bugger I wouldn't have fucked her." I sat down and picked a croissant out of the little basket.

"Oh, you bugger, I don't know." Robyn put her elbows on the table, and I noticed once again that her hands were purely beautiful, just like the rest of her. "I don't know. Some sodomites are amazingly versatile." She smiled, folded the newspaper.

"You have a versatile, perverse mind."

"I know, darling. I know."

"Beaver shots with yogurt. I thought about that."

"I meant you to."

We left the café and walked. The sun was gentle and new.

Robyn took my arm. "Will you marry me?"

We walked, arm in arm. A bus passed, hissing on the pavement. It stopped, people got on, got off, a light changed. We stopped and stood close together. The air smelled fine. The air smelled as if life could begin all over again. I felt we were living in a different decade, the twenties maybe. Hemingway should be here, I thought. This is where things begin, I thought, this is where things end.

"Yes," I said. "Yes, I will."

"That's ever so nice." She held me tighter. "The best birthday present ever."

"It's your birthday?"

"Yes."

"I forgot! And you didn't tell me."

"No, I didn't."

"Well, Happy Birthday."

"Aries," she said. "You should remember. You even made a joke once. Remember?" The light changed again. We crossed the street and we stopped and looked at some books and some 1920s dirty postcards in a bookstall: overweight naked women with fuzzy hair lolling in overstuffed armchairs in sepia. Then Robyn took my arm and we went down the stone steps to the quay.

It was April in Paris.

A *bateau mouche* passed in the narrow channel. The guide's voice echoed in Italian under the arched bridges. Above us floated Notre Dame, its spires dizzy and pure against the cloudless sky. The big cobblestones of the quay were wet and bright in the sun, and there were pigeons and there were easels with painters wearing berets standing in front of them.

The barge with the tearoom on it sloshed up and down, jostling in the wake of the *bateau mouche*. Pigeons flew, whirling—bright flapping splotches—into the sun. Lunch, it said on the hand-painted panel, would cost us seventy-five francs.

Years later we returned to Paris. We wanted to revisit what we had been. We wanted to drop in on our old selves. We wanted to rediscover all those streets, all those plane trees, all those cobblestones, all those glasses of white wine, and all those oysters.

The nuns were still walking within the high walls. The Eiffel Tower was still lit at night. The mist still swirled around Sacré-Coeur. The *bateaux mouches* still plied the echoing channel under Notre Dame. And on the quays old men and young women still sold second-hand books and sepia postcards.

But Margot and Roger, Julie and Pierre-Henri, Sylvie and Marie-Aude, and the golden girl whose wrists were double scarred and whose name I never knew—they were all gone.

The scars, they are me.

But you cannot understand. You are whole.

Now it is night and we are drinking white wine and eating oysters.

"People are so ephemeral, aren't they?" Robyn pushes her dark glasses up, away from her face. She has the most compassionate eyes. "So...transitory."

"Robyn, do you remember?"

"Yes, darling. I remember."

Robyn, sliding an oyster into her mouth, smiles her vague, nostalgic smile, her face half turned to the busy, damp street, the bright, hard Parisian night.

I follow her glance. The red light changes to green. A bus goes past. A man in a flapping tan raincoat runs for it. And for a moment I am nowhere and everywhere, all at once.

Soon, I knew, it would rain. After all, it was April and we were in Paris.

Irony Is . . .

THIS IS A PLACE ON THE EDGE OF THE EARTH.
It's a place strangely unlike a real place. It is an abandoned,
inhuman place, a place of screeching gulls and scorpions
and rocky things. It is an elemental place, a place of
earth and water and air, and fire too—fire from the sky, fire
from the earth, smouldering volcanic rock, *fumaroli* hissing
forth hot steam. It is here. It is now.

It is then.

"Irony is about being in more than one place at a time."
With her finger she twists the curl of blond hair at the edge
of her cheek; she looks at me sideways.

On the horizon there is no sign of anything human, just
the steep slopes of two volcanic peaks, conic and green and
forested, half sunk in the sea. Twin ruins, they make up
another island, at least ten kilometres away from the island
where we find ourselves, suddenly, standing on the beach.

"Interesting," I say. "Interesting concept."

She turns away, looks out to sea. "Professor
Strabiniski's talk on Flaubert was very suggestive," she says
in French, "particularly the part about changing and manip-
ulating the point of view."

"Yes. Sometimes it is awkward."

"Changing a point of view?"

"Yes."

"Yes, it is." She smiles. "Changing one's point of view can be difficult. Depends on the technique, doesn't it?"

"Yes."

For a few moments we don't say anything.

A motorboat had dropped us off, five shipwrecked polyglot professors of literature, five Robinson Crusoes for an afternoon. Except by boat, there is no way to reach this particular beach, or to escape from it. The boat would come back in four hours and pick us up, so the boatman said. Otherwise we would have to spend the night. Or, I muse, we might drown swimming to the next island, or die climbing the cliffs, or dehydrate, or starve to death, or whatever. The naked world, however beautiful, is a cruel place—particularly for five marooned professors of literature.

So this was paradise. Nowhere at all. Everywhere.

She was wearing a pale cream string bikini.

I'd noticed her on the first day of the conference—"Story-Tellers and Stories: Narrative as Weltanschauung"—sitting by the window, in the former convent overlooking the island's port. Like me, she was listening to a boring talk, "Irony in Stendhal's *Chartreuse de Parme*."

It was then that I had had my epiphany—or, in more secular terms, my intimation of lust at first glimpse.

Slouched down in her seat in the third row of the lecture hall, she had a pert boyish profile, ash-blond hair curling down the nape of her neck. She took desultory notes, a quick, casual short-hand scribble, biting her lower lip now and again, and I guessed she knew the subject as well as — or better than — the speaker. At the end of the talk she asked several pointed, but polite, questions. When she stood up, I noticed that her skirt was very short and her legs were very good. She was tactful and gentle with the speaker, who was not nearly as articulate or as well read as she; she didn't press her advantage; she allowed him a gracious retreat. Still, it was a humiliation.

"Do you mind? Would you put some cream on my back?" Again, she says it in the ageless androgynous little girl's voice some French women have.

I smooth on the cream, up under the strap, back down to the small of her back, over her hips. The bikini is so small, so pale, it gives the impression she is naked. Her body is slender and smooth and hard.

After the talk, during coffee, I went over to her and told her I liked her questions and admired her tact and her kindness to the outmanoeuvred speaker. She looked at me from under black eyelashes.

Later that night we had drinks in the hotel bar. She told me she had written a number of learned articles: "Irony and Eros in Laurence Sterne's *Tristram Shandy*," "Pierre Choderlos de Laclos: Paradigm of the Libertine Imagination," "Irony, Desire, and the Master-Slave Dialectic in Hegel's Aesthetic."

These were promising subjects.

The next morning, after the session "The Picaresque as Inner Voyage," we went for a walk in the port. We stood at the quayside and looked down into the dirty water. Metres down, the jellyfish — small, mildly poisonous medusas — pulsated slowly, drifting and colourful in the depths. They sting and can briefly paralyze, but they don't kill, not usually, not unless you are allergic, unusually sensitive, or unlucky. The hot midday reflections flickered like greasy gold coins on the oily water. The brightness made me feel I wanted to go to sleep. Metres down, in depths pierced by the mote-filled rays of the sun, the bottom was a khaki sludge, a wrack of rusty cables, a collection of oil barrels, old tires, tin cans, and gently undulating white plastic shopping bags.

"Not exactly paradise." She made a moue of distaste.

"No."

"If people live in paradise, they invariably destroy it."

"That's so."

"A Hell in Heaven's despite," she said.

"Yes," I said, dazzled by the light, mentally already dozing.

"We can escape," she said. Gold reflections flickered on her face, necklaces of light, tattooed prison bars.

"Escape?" I blinked, woke up. Marble and gold, she seemed a nymph, or a pixie, her eyes emptied, blinded, by the sun.

"We can go to one of the other islands." She pointed at a fisherman on the wharf. Dressed in sharp white and blue, he was bending over, coiling some rope. "He rents boats. He can take us."

So, two hours later, we were stranded with three other

professors on a deserted pebble beach—the edge and the
end of the world.

When you think, when you remember, time shifts.
     Each person is in a different place.
     Always.
     Irony is being in more than one place at one time.
     One single time.
     Pinpoint time. *Tick, tock, tick, tock, tick, tock* . . .
     I said . . .
     He said . . .

"Brrrr!" Professor Ravelli is wearing oversized red-and-black
plaid trunks that sway down from his hairy belly, spilling out
water as he struggles up out of the sea, the pebbles under his
feet rolling, slipping, sliding. His knees are thin, knobby,
his skin etiolated white, streaked with the dark hair streaming.
     "I took Ezra Pound to a beach near Ravenna once," he
says.
     "Yes?" She smiles at him over her shoulder, smooth
shoulder glow of cream, oil, sun, slender backbone curving,
gentle ass rising: a melody, in time, in space.
     "Yes. Then near Rapallo. We drank white wine."
     "White wine? Really?"
     "Indeed, and—"
     "Professor! Can you help me?" Signorina Vecchio is the
professor's assistant; she is his creature; ostentatiously she
worships her master. She is short, with enormous breasts

and a handsome, heavily sensual Roman face. Academic rumour has it that Signorina Vecchio sleeps with Professor Ravelli; the jealous claim that she owes her contract at the university solely to the professor's insistent intervention on her behalf—that's what they say, "insistent intervention."

"Poets and madmen," says Professor Ravelli, looking up at the sun. He reaches out to help the signorina as she struggles on the slippery pebbles. Wet, her one-piece red bathing suit seems transparent, paints her nudity a gaudy scarlet. She smiles brightly, worshipfully, at Professor Ravelli. "Poets and madmen. Under the midday sun, my dear." He smiles; a broken tooth gleams.

"Mad dogs and Englishmen. *Idiot*," mutters my French nymph. She turns a page: Rimbaud.

> *O saisons, ô châteaux*
> *Quelle âme est sans défaut!*

The light flutters as she turns another page.

> *Oisive jeunesse*
> *A tout asservie,*
> *Par délicatesse*
> *J'ai perdu ma vie.*

Up in a narrow strip of shade, dangerously close under the cliff, Professor Hobbes lies on his belly turning the pages of a thick French book, *The AntiOedipus*.

Hobbes is English, misanthropic, and timid, with pimples on his back and an unsuccessful red beard. His accent is of uncertain provenance and pretentious intent. He is offhand to the point of idiocy.

"*Imbécile*," opines my French nymph.

Then she says: "Sometimes when things happen, in memory, it seems they happened to somebody else, but then you realize that they happened to you." She leans back and smiles. "I imagine you've had that experience."

She really does look like a boy, with her candid, lightly tanned face, her very precise lips, precise just as all of her neat, self-contained, carefully sculpted Gallic person is precise.

"Yes. Yes, I have," I say.

Lazily I am aflame, and I wonder if her androgyny ignites a partially sublimated tendency to pedophilia, or homosexuality, or perhaps a sort of Peter Pan nostalgia for my own androgynous past, my childhood, when it seemed I could have or be anything or anybody, man, woman, king, pauper. None of this matters. Whatever ignites the moment will, I suppose, serve.

"Sex is a matter of intelligence," she says. "As much intelligence as of anything else." She is holding a small rounded, dusty pebble between thumb and forefinger, examining it. "Don't you think?"

"Sex in the head is all in the mind."

"Obviously." From over her shoulder, she smirks. "Tautological."

"Pleonastic, *mon chèr ami*. Redundant like an obsession, like a perversion. The poor old Marquis de Sade, for instance, can't help repeating himself. He keeps chewing at the same old bones, the same old cud. Even the *Histoire d'O* is obsessive in its repetitions." She runs the point of her tongue along her lip, puts the little round pebble carefully down to nest in her bellybutton. "Fetishistic desire — perhaps all desire — is asymptotic, I think: it forever approaches, but never reaches, its fleeing object, its retreating goal."

"The real object being incestuous, therefore taboo?"

"Perhaps. Freud, at least, would have it so." Her voice trails off, dreamy, absent.

We are pleased with this routine; together we can play any number of variants. It's like a dance or a piano duo: puerile and pointless but vaguely arousing.

There is a silence. Professor Ravelli and Signorina Vecchio are examining something at the far end of the beach. The cliffs curve up, threatening, high above them.

Pale and alone in his strip of shadow, Professor Hobbes coughs, says something amazed like "This is the most incredible shit!" But we are not really meant to hear, I think, or we are not meant to acknowledge that we have heard. Tonight at the official dinner he will tell us what shit it is and will mumble why precisely it is such shit while he stares at the tablecloth and pushes breadcrumbs around with the point of his knife. Not all of what he says will be idiotic.

"Tautologies do express something," she says, suddenly becoming serious. "There is a semantic value in redundancy, different angles on the same thing. A different universe is brought to bear when you use a synonym, a so-called synonym." She pushes a strand of hair from her eyes.

"Yes."

"Different contexts." She shades her eyes. "You recontextualize continually when you talk, when you think. Since no term—in natural languages, at least—is ever entirely synonymous with any other term, the pleonastic is not really pleonastic, so you are continually evoking whole semantic universes, family resemblances, contextual genealogies. If you wish to consider connotations and contexts, of course."

"Yes," I murmur. She is interesting, I think, really interesting.

"Abstract thought requires decontextualization, and recontextualization. You have to take what is relevant from one context and transport it to another context. I've been thinking about it a lot. The physical, the corporeal, correlates of creativity."

"Yes." I like looking at her when she frowns.

"You have to be in different places at once: mental places, physical places, thinking yourself into different universes, different contexts."

"Yes." I close my eyes and try to visualize it—hmm, different universes, different contexts. Let's see: now I am Signorina Vecchio, heavy breasted and dripping salt water. No, I'm not sure I want to do that. Now I am Professor

Ravelli, leaning lasciviously towards Signorina Vecchio and dreaming of drinking wine with Ezra Pound. No, that I can pass on—definitely. Now I am Ezra Pound, figuring out—decades ago now—what to make of Professor Ravelli. No—too difficult. And now? Now, best of all, I am a round, hot pebble, snuggled in the nymph's bellybutton.

"You have to appreciate the nuance of different levels of discourse, different social contexts, different conceptual contexts or sensory contexts or temporal contexts or mental sets. These are all different conceptual models that you superimpose. Like the light brilliantly strumming the sea in that poem by...I've forgotten. I think it was Stephen Spender. The image—light strumming the sea—is a transposition, a metaphor." She smiles, suddenly sheepish, looking down, moving the pebble from her bellybutton. "I apologize. I'm giving one of my lectures."

"No apologies needed. I find this positively inebriating."

"Inebriating?" She smiles again, moving the pebble back so it cradles once more in her bellybutton, a polished smoky jewel in a warm whorl, a tiny maelstrom of young flesh.

And so it went. In those days it seemed so important to know ourselves, and each other. Through the analysis of texts we would understand ourselves, and the world. Through the study of texts we would reinvent everything. Even ourselves. We, after all, were "texts" too, inscriptions and palimpsests, where traces of every single event ever were left to be found, to be read, to be savoured.

Adam and Eve drunk in the knowledge of texts.

We were beautiful once.
   Sure. Sure you were.
   We were clever too.
   Sure. Sure you were.
   I mean "we," all of us.
   Sure, you were. Sure, we were. All of us.

I'm telling the story to somebody in a bar; I don't really know if I know this person. It is many years later, and I am drunk, maybe, but I don't really know. A long time ago I ceased knowing whether I was drunk or not, or when, or how. Outside this bar it is snowing. I think it is snowing. Maybe it's stopped, I don't know. All the sounds, anyway, are muffled. It's like being deaf. Could be it's summer outside this bar, high summer, for all I know, and all the birds are twittering.

She was beautiful.
   Yeah, I'll bet.

Some people don't believe in anything—no ideals, no faith, no past, no future. You know, that's what the world has come to, or that's what this life has come to. No interest either, not in anything. Today, we are all *cool*, however hot it might be.

Outside maybe it's raining, maybe it's snowing.

New York—I think today I'm in New York.

It is bitter cold and dry; sharp stars are in the sky, even above Manhattan. They are singing Christmas carols at

Rockefeller Center. The Rockettes are probably dancing. People, muffled up, are skating on the small rink. I've been drunk there, in Manhattan, and walked the long straight cold windy streets, and looked up, seeing my breath sweep away...

Heat and humidity blaze down, white, out of the sky. My skin drips; everything is soaked. The pebbles glow white.

Soon a storm will break.

Maybe we'll be caught in the hot rain. Maybe the boat won't make it back. Maybe we'll shelter in each other's arms, under the curve of the cliff, alone. I would like to embrace her and hold her. I look up at the sky.

"In any situation, we are more than just who we are." She is speaking over her shoulder. White curve of smooth oiled shoulder, catching the light.

"Uh-huh."

"I mean, like when I make love I like to imagine, say, that I'm a whore..." Again she turns over on her back, and levers herself up on her elbows—flat belly, cupcake breasts, triangles of cream cloth, chalk-white collarbone carved in light. She looks at me from under her thick black eyelashes—enough to make you dizzy.

"Uh-huh." I pick up a pebble, afraid to look at her.

"So, I'm a whore, a *pute*, a trollop, a fuck, an easy fuck, a cunt, cheap tail, two-bit ass, whatever...I feel it, I am, I make myself, every inch of me, into a whore. I am that idea, the idea I create. You understand?"

"Uh-huh. Yes." I look up, straight into her eyes staring back at me, serious, not laughing at all.

"You pick me up on the street. Maybe, say, rue Saint-Denis in Paris, or Place Pigalle. Or maybe I'm sitting at a bar, maybe we're in Texas. I'm sitting on one of those really high bar stools, you know, net stockings, plastic miniskirt, gold spike heels. I am drunk with my own cheapness, with my display. It's all in my mind. You see?"

"I see. Clearly, I see." I close my eyes; I open them again.

She blinks, glances away at Professor Ravelli, wading waist-deep in the pale blue. He looks fragile, pale and insubstantial, as if the soft-breathing smoky blue water might easily break him in two. Farther out, Signorina Vecchio is splashing, cavorting, and gushing, like a young porpoise.

"But I'm another part of me too, another person. I am I imagining me being a whore. I'm object and subject. I'm male and female, exhibitionist and voyeur, director and actress. I script and frame myself. See what I mean?"

"I think so."

"He thinks so." She smiles a crafty smile, and the tip of her tongue moves along her lip. She laughs.

In one gracious unfolding of legs and body, she stands up, catching the umbilical pebble, saving it in her curled hand. "You are a funny man, and I like you."

I stand up.

She takes my arm as if we had been doing this for decades—the top of her head is even with my chin—and we walk down along the pebbled beach to join Professor Ravelli and Signorina Vecchio.

Up in the one strip of shade, Professor Hobbes, still lying on his belly, turns a page of his book. "Shit!" he says.

"The water is wonderful." Professor Ravelli raises his skinny arm, beckons us in.

The water was wonderful.

The boat came and we were not shipwrecked after all.

That evening, after a lavish fifteen-course Sicilian meal, the conference broke up. The next morning, when I came down with my bags, she had already left. But in my box, in a sealed perfumed envelope, was a message. "I like you very much. We shall meet again."

For many months I had no news of her. But the image remained, and I thought of her almost every day. When you first see a woman you desire—or maybe it's a man— you remember exactly what you saw, exactly how you saw her—or him. Everything is etched as in a tableau—gesture, clothes, lighting, expression, eyes, lips, smile or frown, the inner tension, the outer luminosity or darkness—everything is etched in the mind. At least for me, that's the way it is.

Then one day, in Rome, where I lived, she phoned. She was coming to Rome: would I have lunch with her?

So we had lunch, out on the terrace of a restaurant. It was a hot day with rain threatening. We drank and we talked and I was excited because, as the luncheon progressed, it was evident she wanted to go home to my place and go to bed with me. Her hair was shorter and she was even more boyish, more cool and yet intense, than before. Love—or desire—is something you fall into, like an abyss.

We talked of love and sex and desire; there were many teasing innuendoes and quirky suggestions, horizons of good-humoured depravity, of psychological intricacy, of intimacies undreamed of.

Those were the days when dreams thronged, when dreams were easy and cheap, when dreams had the energy that made them come true.

We drank three bottles of wine and then started on a bottle of vodka.

She went into the restaurant. To the lady's room, I presumed. I felt the heat on my skin and drank more vodka. The vodka was cold, sweetly antiseptic, thick, slow moving like glue. I licked the frozen poison. She came back to the table.

"He's here."

"Who?"

"My husband, the Judge."

"Husband?"

"Yes." She smiled.

"The Judge, your husband, is here. Where here?" I looked around. She hadn't told me about a husband.

"In Rome."

"Your husband's a judge?"

"For the Boy Scouts."

"I didn't know..." I didn't know the Boy Scouts ran an Inquisition, I thought.

"No. Silly!"

"Now I'm silly."

"Don't be upset. He's coming to join us."

"The Judge?"

"Yes." She leaned forward, bare elbows on the table, delicate muscular arms. "He's here, in Rome, for the Boy Scouts. He's on the national committee."

"Of the Boy Scouts."

"Yes." She looked at me carefully. Eyes like grey novas. The intelligence of the whole universe, of all of the cosmos, of God himself, was right there, in those eyes, focused on me.

"We'll go to your place." She ran the tip of her tongue along her upper lip.

"Yeah, but..."

"We'll make love. You and I." She smiled: it was a sad smile, ever so slightly sad. "You and I will fuck."

"We will?" It's what I was planning to do, what I wanted to do.

"Yes. We will fuck. Shall fuck."

"But..."

"He won't mind."

"Ah."

"In fact..." She stopped, looked across the little square. Two children were skipping against the wall opposite us; it was a beautiful ochre wall, covered in thick ivy. The afternoon heat glowered down. Soon it would rain. Our bodies were coated in hot sweat.

I waited.

"In fact..." Her fingers drummed for an instant on the tablecloth, slender, nails unpainted, beautifully manicured.

"Go on."

"In fact..." Her eyes looked straight at mine, her tongue ran along her lower lip, she bit her lip.

"I'm listening."

"It's the only way he...can enjoy...I mean the only way he can feel...things."

"Knowing you are fucking?"

"Seeing. Watching."

"Ah."

"Otherwise he can't..."

"Ah." Slowly my mind began to put some pieces together. "I see. He likes to see. To watch. You and somebody else."

"Yes."

"Well." What, I wondered, does Anglo-Saxon honour and bravado dictate in such a situation?

"He can't...he can't have sex...not normally, I mean. He hasn't...Not for a long time."

"And you?"

"Well...I..." She shrugged, bit her lip.

"I see." I poured us both more vodka. The owner of the restaurant, Roberto, waved and smiled from where he was standing in the doorway. The lunch crowd was winding

down, and he'd just escaped from the kitchen. If I wasn't so
obviously involved in an intense conversation, he would
have come over and joined us, he would have sat down with
his elbows on the table, and we would have enjoyed some
gossip. But he sensed something was happening and disappeared back inside. "I see," I said. I clicked my glass against
hers. "You know, I like you very much," I said. "I think I'm
almost in love."

She clinked her glass against mine. Looking me in the
eye, she emptied her glass. Her smile made her look about
twelve years old.

"No," I said, "I *am* in love."

The Judge arrived in a cab. He was very pleasant and
drank some vodka and we talked about the new government budget and whether it would get through Parliament
intact or be modified by too many amendments to serve the
purpose for which...

The Judge paid for lunch.

"The Judge will sit in the corner." She paces the bedroom
like a stage director, and points. "Over there."

"Okay." I move a chair over to the corner. The Judge
looks at the chair, then looks at me. I nod.

The Judge sits in the corner. He is a paunchy man with
a set of premature jowls. Everything is grey—his hair is
grey, his stubble is grey, his skin has a sickly slick, wet, grey
pallor. The Judge is not old, but he looks old.

It rains, sporadically, big hot drops against the closed bedroom window.

"Mind if I smoke?" The Judge looks at me with half-closed eyes.

"No."

The Judge takes out a cigar. Carefully, he unwraps it. The plastic crackles in the quiet room. Slowly, he licks the cigar, up and down.

"We undress now," she says. Arms akimbo, she looks around the room, surveying the stage: everything appears to be in order. She frowns.

"Okay. We undress. He watches?"

She nods.

I look at the Judge, and he nods too.

I take off my shirt and then unbuckle my jeans. If I weren't so stubborn, or so drunk, I wouldn't be doing this. I sit down on the edge of the bed to undo my shoelaces. The room is filling with the heavy blue cigar smoke. I get up and in stocking feet I go over and open the window. Beyond the iron bars of the window, grey slanting rain streaks down. The air from outside drifts in, wet and hot and fresh against my face.

She's barefoot, down to panties, little white bikini panties with a tiny frill running at the bottom edge. I wonder if she bought them thinking of him, thinking of how they would please him, of how they would please the Judge. My child, my love: *mon enfant, mon amour.*

"Keep that. Keep that for a while," says the Judge. He waves the cigar at the frilly triangle of white.

She turns and stretches, her arms up in the air, wrists crossed, just like I'd seen her do on the beach. A quarter-pirouette, ankles crossed. The kind of divinely smooth movement that made somebody invent nymphs.

"But him, I want him naked." The Judge waves the cigar in my direction. A slow, lazy swirl of smoke. "If you don't mind," he says to me.

The cigar smoke hangs like a blue cloud.

Behind the cloud the Judge is a grey-silver lump, a melted-down monument. The smoke hangs thicker; no light is lit in the room; everything seems to be taking place on a ghostly backlit stage. We are coated in slippery silver-grey shadow.

I let my jeans drop, step out of my socks. She reaches out for them. Is this part of the ritual? Is she my handmaiden? I hand her the jeans and socks; she leans down, picks up the shoes, stands—waits. She looks like a waitress waiting for an order, or, in a strange way, like a pageboy, a naked page-boy. Her body is smooth, white, totally hairless. I wonder what's under the panties, whether she's all smooth.

I step out of my underpants and hand them over.

The Judge breathes out a big cloud of smoke. I guess he's sizing me up.

She takes the bundle of clothes—hers and mine—and disappears out the door. This way we will be naked, truly naked. The Judge and I are alone. I wonder a little bit about the Judge, but mostly I wonder about her. The Judge half closes his eyes, squints at me, puffs on his cigar. It almost looks like he is about to fall asleep. The blue smoke fills the air.

"Your honour, I wonder if I might..."

"You climb on top of me," she says.

I already have an erection. I don't like to mention it, but I do. It's one of those drunk dark days when I'm totally outside myself and totally inside myself too, hungry and lusty and sick with yearning for her and for the theatricality of the entire perverse situation.

I climb on top of her.

"Good."

The thing is, as she instructs and explains to me, the thing is, I am to mime copulation by holding her down, by crushing her, and by rubbing my erection as hard as I can against her panties, against her. I rub hard and I hold her down tight on the hard mattress. My cock is hard and her panties are hot and wet so at least I know we are both participating. I look over my shoulder.

The judge sits slumped back in the chair in the corner, his eyes half-closed, smoking his cigar, almost asleep.

"Tell me stuff." She wets her lips.

"Stuff?"

"Dirty kinky weird stuff." The eyes, cat's eyes now, blink.

I try out a few things; they don't work. She explains, as we rub against each other—she is under me and I am on top of her—and as we move our hands over each other and as our mouths meet and bite and lick and touch—that I'm supposed to whisper gruff kinky cruel tales of forcible bodily metamorphosis.

"Ah..."

"Understand?"

"Uh-huh."

"Like *Freaks*?"

"Yes. Like Tod Browning. Like *Freaks*."

I propose a tale of total body tattooing with multiple piercings. She will be tattooed and pierced, head to toe, rings and chains hanging everywhere, and displayed in a cage in an itinerant circus. This excites her a bit but not really enough. At first she was passive, lying limp and almost rigid under me; now she is clinging to me, licking, searching. I really like her; the only thing I don't like is that her skin is impregnated with the Judge's cigar smoke. The man seeps from her every pore. She clings tighter and tighter.

"Every time you have an orgasm, you turn just a little bit into a monkey." I'm inspired.

"A monkey?"

"Uh-huh. Every time you get excited, hair grows, all over."

She wiggles. "I like that. Where does the hair grow?"

I close her mouth with my mouth to up the ante, to heighten the suspense.

A puff of approving cigar smoke drifts over us. Who, I wonder, is in control here?

"Where does it grow?" Her voice is a gruff whisper against my shoulder.

"Everywhere. On your back, on your shoulders and arms."

She begins to undulate, pushing her pelvis up against mine.

"On your legs."

She wiggles, tighter and tighter. The panties are wet, soaked, straining against my erection.

"Up your belly, the hair creeps. Down your cheeks, it sprouts on your chin."

"Oh!"

She wiggles more; her mouth is hot. Her hand slides down my side, she takes hold of me, forcing her hand in between us, and squeezes. Then she hooks a finger of her other hand under her panties and begins to rub herself.

"Talk! Don't stop!" Her voice teeters on the edge of a throaty cry. In her white throat, titled back, a blue vein pulses. She is trembling.

"Your body is slowly covering, slowly, slowly covering in thick black fur..."

With her thumbs she hooks her panties, begins to push them down, her arms so close to her sides she's armless. Her beautiful tight shoulders gleaming in sweat, she gyrates under me, her muscular white body hard against mine. Overhead some jets streak by. The roar echoes in the small courtyard outside the bedroom window. The pigeons flutter and whirl up. The Judge's cigar smoke drifts out through the open window, out through the iron prison bars, out into the gently slanting hush of the rain. Each drop has a distinct and separate sound, hitting a roof tile, a cobblestone, a stucco wall, a glass-topped terrace table, the waxen leaf of a flower, the serrated frond or the petal of a rose, the clay or pebbles or fine sand of a window box.

She is licking my lips, kissing, whispering uncontrollable, indistinguishable, indecipherable, inaudible words — a string of mad hot crazy damp vodka-perfumed words. Her right foot kicks slowly free of the panties, working it off one ankle and then the other. She has very slender ankle bones, I think. Very delicate, fragile ankle bones. I whisper about the dark, thick fur spreading, thickening, darkening in her armpits and along her arms. She shudders and brings her hand in to guide me into her, though I don't need much guiding. She is wide open, liquid, and as I slip into her she vibrates with a throbbing little whispered cry and goes into her first orgasm. The Judge coughs. I think, soon I will die. She shudders, stretches, shudders, stretching under me, her hands now wrapped around my back, her legs coming up, scissors-like, crossing tight over my back.

"Do I have a tail?"

"Pardon?"

"A tail. Do I have a tail?" She laughs close in my ear, lips brushing my ear, tongue licking, brushing.

"Oh, yeah. You have a long thin snaky smooth hairy monkey tail."

This sends her into another shudder, eyes closed. She

vibrates and trembles as if she were being torn apart. I ride
her, hold her, clasp her tight and realize something that I had
not realized before: her sex has been shaved or waxed
smooth, prepubescent smooth, the way she was meant to be.

"Your bush drips honey," I whisper, biting into her ear,
remembering something I had read somewhere.

She shivers and heads for another orgasm.

"Do I hang by my tail?" A breathless whisper.

"Honey, you swing from every branch with your tail,
you're an acrobat with your tail, nobody's got a better, more
prehensile tail than you. You're a regular circus monkey."

The sole of my left foot tickles. There must be a fly. I try
to kick it away. I look over my shoulder. It's the Judge—
he's on his hands and knees next to the bed like a large
grey-flannel dog. "What the hell—!"

"Shhhh!" She puts her hand over my mouth.

"Glllumpph?"

"He wants to tickle your feet."

"Glllumpph? Tickle my—?"

"Shhhh!"

"I don't—"

"Shhhh!

"I don't want him fooling around with my fucking feet!"

"Shhhhh! Don't use bad words."

"Well..."

Tickle, tickle, tickle...

"He won't mind if you kick a bit," she whispers into my
ear. So I kick a bit. I can hear the Judge giggling and

twittering to himself, and making little sucking noises, and then...

The rest is just snapshots. She is a smooth-haired monkey hanging by her tail from a light bulb in the living room. She is a smooth-haired monkey and we are fucking on the tiled red roof out beyond the window. She and I are both smooth-haired long-tailed monkeys chittering amiably to each other high in a tropical banana tree. Close by is the azure of an exotically smooth ocean, a plate of cobalt glass. We are so intimate, she and I, chittering away meaninglessly, that we would pick fleas out of each other's pelts if we had fleas, but we don't have fleas, because this is paradise. I hand her a banana and she rewards me with a monkey kiss...She and I are human again, married, living into old age, having many children. She and I are in a circus, our act is famous, indeed, throughout the Middle East. She and I are inside a suburb inside a white picket fence, wearing double-breasted pinstriped suits, watering petunias and smoking cheroots.

The Judge sits in a cloud of smoke, collapsed like a tired, depleted grey Buddha. I'm on my knees in front of her and it's true she's not a monkey at all. She's a temple, an ogive, and a sacrament. Now I'm on top of her and now she's a recently captured slave girl covered in the Mediterranean sweat and the sunset glow of the Barbary Coast. Now, hair shorn short, she's a cabin boy, newly embarked, virginal arms muddied with fresh tar. *Yo, ho, ho, and a bottle of rum, and let me peg it to you, laddie...*

Then somehow we are out in the street, she, the Judge, and yours truly. All three of us are dressed and we look quite a bit like human beings. The Judge lights a cigar and the rain has disappeared so there is no need for umbrellas. The Judge puffs on his cigar and looks at the ash at the end.

We go for a walk. Following the Judge's instructions, she and I walk ahead, arm-in-arm, while the Judge strolls behind, keeping a benevolent eye on us.

"I'm sorry," she says, leaning into me.

"Don't be."

We sit down inside the Café Greco in Via Condotti. It is a fashionable place, frequented by Japanese tourists, Italian designers, bankers, and a few aging artists.

The first Italian Republic is nearing its end, or so it seems, and I am tempted to see some apocalyptic sense in what has happened, but I don't. Terrorists have been shooting politicians, businessmen, and judges. Bombs blow up trains, banks, and supermarkets. Children are shot down in a splash of blood on the steps of synagogues. Students and poets are clubbed to death. Shots ring out at night. Prime ministers are kidnapped, shot dead, left as crumpled, bloody corpses in the trunks of small cars. It's a usual occurrence to be frisked at night at a roadblock, you in black tie, your hands up, and your girl in high heels, her hands flat on the roof of the car, leaning forward, in a strapless gown, long, tanned legs spread, straining, head down, hair cascading. "Is this going to make us late at the Ambassador's?" "No, I don't think so." "Sorry, madam." "Go ahead, help yourself." Hands slide up her legs, down her sides, down her bodice. A bomb can hide anywhere. A world is coming to an end, or so it seemed. But this too was an exaggeration — like everything else in those years.

The president of the republic is almost ninety years old. He suddenly appears in the café, sits at a table opposite us, and is immediately surrounded by young Japanese girls clamouring to be photographed. The president's dentures grin. He puts his arm around two young Japanese women. Flashes flash. The president is bald, has mummified sun-mottled dark skin, and looks like an amiable mummy resurrected from a tomb. For more than a decade he had been a political prisoner, exiled to an island prison. His eyes stare out from thick round glasses. The president looks around; his eyes take us in; his head nods. He sips at his espresso.

We are out in the street.

The Judge shakes my hand. "Next time we shall talk of politics," he says. "The president is a great man," he says, motioning with his cigar.

She kisses me on the cheeks, then, chastely, softly, slowly, on the lips, her hand against the side of my face.

For a moment they are at the corner of the street, silhouetted against the Spanish Steps, against the Piazza di Spagna, and the freshly washed late-afternoon sky. They turn the corner, and they are gone.

Time is suddenly unreal, shifts gears and carries me else-where, into a new zone. I am drunk, still drunk. It is instantaneous twilight, the time of transitions and voyages, of homecomings and returns, the hour of the day when you realize you have no home to go home to. I look up at the chunk of sky stuck between the cornices of Via Condotti. There are no clouds, just the darkening Mediterranean blue. It's a blue so fine it makes you blind. Such perfection is unbearable.

So where do I go and what do I do now that I have done everything that can be imagined? I am still drunk, hung over and drunk at the same time, which is a very bad state to be in.

Irony, she said, is seeing yourself from outside, seeing yourself on a stage.

No, no—that's not what she said. What she said was... yes, what she said was, irony is being in more than one place at once, in more than one place at one and the same time.

People are busy shopping, hurrying to appointments, trysts, assignations. I have the odour of cigars and sex on me. I came, but outside her, as was agreed with the Judge, and now here I am in my jeans and T-shirt, in the middle of the street, depleted, reeking of sex, at the beginning of a fine warm evening.

What do I do now?

What do you do when you die?

I'm in love with the kinky monkey girl. No, not really, that's not quite right. I like her a lot. She's as sexy and sweet and smart as anyone I know, and I'm curious about her life with the Judge. How do they live? Out in the country? Near the small university town where they both work? What do they talk about at night? What do they do? Does she bring boys home...?

I stop at a bar and have another drink. I'm horny. All my higher and baser instincts aroused yet unslaked.

I set off on one of those endless evenings and nights of drinking, heading from bar to bar, phoning women I know and women I hardly know and women I don't know.

My senses are sharpened. Being a post-coital drunk on a fine warm blue evening can be a religious experience. I feel used, of course. I feel betrayed. I feel like shit. I feel good too, like I pulled something off. Maybe, I think, the Judge will love her just a bit more; maybe he'll despise her just a bit more. Maybe he's happy, the Judge, or maybe he's sad. And then I wonder, for a moment, who the Judge was when she and I made love. Himself? Her? Me? Somebody else? Everybody at once?

I figure it doesn't matter, except for him, for them.

Irony is being in more than one place at a time.

I put the coins in the slot and push the buttons and listen to the number ring.

It rings and rings and rings.

I hang up. I'm on a street corner. I don't know what street corner I'm on, or what streets these are. A moon has come up, an unrepentant, full, masturbatory moon.

La lune ne garde aucune rancune.

I never heard from the monkey girl again. Not from the Judge either. We never did discuss politics.

Years later I tried to find the monkey girl and the Judge. I even visited the small university town where they'd told me they lived. I gave a lecture. There was a cocktail party. I met many people. I walked up and down streets. I looked in the phone book. I questioned members of the faculty. I looked up the records. That night I ate alone at a corner table in a small restaurant near the station, drank a bottle of strong red wine and wondered about life. I was strangely elated.

So this, I thought, is paradise.

So this, I thought, is irony.

Sitting on the edge of the hotel bed, I phoned Professor Ravelli. "Professor, do you remember that day on the beach, that day when we went out—?"

"Oh, yes, with that charming Professor Hobbes. Have you read his translation of—?"

"Yes, Professor, but do you remember...?"

No.

No?

No, he didn't remember. Was I sure, was I really sure?

Yes. I was sure. I was really sure.

After I hung up I sat staring at the hotel wallpaper. It was one of those complex designs, stained by years of misuse, a leaky window, an overheated, rusty radiator. In those blotches I saw many things. I drank some more wine, and thought about Professor Hobbes and about Ezra Pound on the beach at Rapallo.

And now, of course, I am in love.

Hey, Mister!

"HEY, MISTER!"

The jeep raced past, leaving behind a cloud of dust. The driver didn't notice the little boy. For a moment the little boy ran alongside the jeep, but then he fell behind.

"Hey, mister!"

The driver was wearing a blue baseball cap and had a thin, sunburnt face that was just a bit too handsome; the blue eyes were narrowed, crinkled against the dust and the sun.

"Hey, mister!"

The voice disappeared behind the jeep, lost in the roar of the motor, the rush of wind, the rising dust.

"Hey, mister!"

I'm no mister, thought the driver, half registering the voice, half seeing the small flickering presence, and glancing now, finally, into the rear-view mirror, where the small boy was a tiny vertical speck, dark, fragile, and lost in the white glare of the dusty road. It must be the cap, thought the driver, it must be the baseball cap, maybe the sunburn and the dirt, maybe the hair. The driver blinked at the rear-view mirror and saw the blue cap pulled down tight, a smear of dirt on the forehead, dust-burnt, sunburnt cheeks, and two very blue eyes, eyes from Europe, eyes from America.

The driver jerked the wheel to the right. The jeep careened, just managed a tight U-turn, tilted dangerously on two wheels, spewed dust and gravel; then it was down with a thud, the four wheels suddenly gripping the broken gravel, spinning, racing in the soft, traitorous dust. The driver stamped on the accelerator. It was dangerous, and it was against the rules. Somewhere the rhythmic crescendo of artillery overtook the roar of the motor. It was subliminal—the distant sound of killing. There was nobody alive on the road, nobody alive in the village, just dead bodies, lots of dead bodies and shattered walls standing in the rubble of what had once been a town.

The driver squinted against the glare. Maybe the little boy had been an illusion. Maybe he didn't exist at all. The driver squinted, wiped at the dust.

No. There he was.

The driver skidded the jeep to a stop. Dust rose.

The little boy looked up, blinked.

POM, POM, POM, POM—the beating of mortar fire. Plaster and stucco fell off a shattered wall. More white dust rising.

POM, POM, POM, POM.

I'm a fool, thought the driver.

"Mister?" said the little boy.

"Hop in. Come on!"

The little boy stared.

"Come on!" The driver wiped away a thick, dusty grease of sweat. "*Viens! Monte!*"

The little boy climbed up.

"Do you speak English?" The driver looked down at the little boy. "English?"

The little boy shrugged. "Hold on tight," said the driver in French. "*Tiens-toi bien!*"

The little boy grabbed the driver's belt and held on.

POM, POM, POM, POM.

The mortars were closer now. Part of a stucco wall fell away; white dust puffed out on the road and rose in waves, moving in slow, silent, and sleepy motion. The driver gunned the jeep; one thin hand pulled the baseball cap tighter.

The road was long and straight and the driver drove hard.

Flies were buzzing. They were stopped at a roadblock. Cars and trucks were lined up; passengers were getting out, holding up their hands, surrendering, like in a spaghetti western. But the soldiers weren't cowboys; the soldiers had big smiles, automatic weapons, machetes, and uniforms that were dark with sweat, dust, and blood. The driver looked at the little boy. There would be trouble. There would probably be trouble. The driver took off the baseball cap and unpinned the long blond hair. It fell to her shoulders.

"I'm no mister," she said.

"Mister?" said the little boy.

"*Non. Une femme. Je suis une femme.*"

"*Une femme,*" said the little boy.

"Yes," said the driver. She was once again glad for her two years at the University of Bordeaux. "Your mother?" she asked. "*Ta mère?*"

The little boy hesitated. Then he drew his finger across his throat.

"Ah," said the driver. She put her hand on the little boy's thick crinkly hair. He was remarkably well dressed.

Behind the soldiers were stacks of bodies, fresh bodies piled up like firewood, gleaming black, mostly naked, with red smears here and there. "Men have died from time to time, and worms have eaten them, but not for love." Why did she think of that, just now? She thought suddenly about Shakespeare and Professor Northrop Frye and the University of Toronto and she wondered about the amorousness of worms.

The line advanced slowly.

She changed gears and advanced up to the roadblock. The soldiers grinned. She smiled back, handed over her passport and documents.

"Canada..."

One of the soldiers had a larger grin than the others; he came up close, narrowing his eyes, took out his machete and slid it under the boy's throat. The little boy sat rigid, his fingers gripping the edge of the seat. The driver glanced at another soldier. His uniform had dark green epaulettes: an officer. She caught his eye and held his gaze. The officer stepped forward, put his hand on the soldier's shoulder. "*Non,*" he said.

The soldier hesitated. The point of the machete was at the little boy's jugular, pressed under his chin. The little boy didn't move, didn't look. He just stared ahead.

The soldier with the machete stepped back. He looked up at the driver, grinned, and ran his forefinger slowly across his throat.

The driver smiled and shook her head very slightly. The soldier nodded.

The officer frowned. "*Allez-y,*" he said. "*Vite.*" Go, get out of here.

Half closing her eyes, the driver gave the officer a lazy salute, put the jeep in gear and accelerated.

They left the checkpoint behind. Dust rose off the road. The driver heard shots, glanced in the rear-view mirror, saw that the soldiers had shot all the passengers in the car behind. She knew it was because of her.

The road was long and straight and the war was for a time left behind. The driver drove fast. Army columns streamed in the opposite direction. Nobody stopped them.

Soon it will be night, the driver thought, noticing the fading light of the sky.

She pulled to the side of the road. Two palms drooped in the dusty air. One shattered wall that had once been something caught the light of the sinking sun. For some reason she thought of an abandoned drive-in movie theatre, the screen still up, grass growing in the asphalt, idle and rusty metal posts for attaching earphones; then she thought of ochre walls in Rome, a little hotel near the Forum, of how you could sit with your elbows on the table drinking coarse white wine from the Castelli and watch the sun set over broken marble columns and cornices. The sky had turned a sharper blue. Soon it would be dark.

"Hungry?" She pulled out a small kit box. "*Tu as faim?*"

The little boy nodded.

She took one of the sandwiches she had carefully packed; she cut it in two and handed the little boy one half. With his little brown hand he took it warily and looked her in the eyes.

"*Merci,*" he said. His voice was barely a whisper.

He is well dressed, she thought, well fed, and he speaks French. Yes, his parents had been part of the élite, the former élite.

She thought of the soldier who had caressed the little boy's neck with the edge of the machete.

She poured some water from the thermos into the thermos cap and handed the full cup to the little boy. He looked up; his eyes were frightened. She placed the cup in his hands and smiled.

"*Ca va mieux, n'est-ce pas?*"

"*Merci,*" he said.

"It's better now," she said, cutting another sandwich, handing half to the little boy.

"*Oui,*" he said.

♦ ♦ ♦

The sun disappeared in an instant, and half an hour later the air was bitter cold. The jeep was pulled over beside an abandoned farmhouse.

The little boy lay against the woman. His body was warm and his skin smelled of dust and sun; her arm was around his shoulder and he cradled against her breast. Her eyes were open and she thought she might count the stars—there were so many, too many. She ran her fingers through her hair; it was long and blond and now clogged and heavy with sweat and dust. How long had it been since she had had a bath, a shower, a shampoo?

The little boy stirred in his sleep, half turned, and snaked his arm in around her waist. She felt the smooth, warm curve of his body and cradled him as if he were her own. She pulled the blanket tighter around both of them and closed her eyes.

The air turned warm. The moon was high and so bright it seemed like a day photographed in negative.

She got up and walked back and forth and then she sat down on the shattered floor, her chin on her knees, staring at the little boy. He was sleeping, or he seemed to be sleeping. She wondered if he had already been trained in deceit, and then she wondered at her own cynicism. She had seen so many die; she had seen so many kill; perhaps her eyes no longer saw anything at all.

She remembered kneeling beside a mother and her dying child. In black-and-white she shot them—it had been very impressive: the skeletal mother, dried flecks of foam at the edges of her chapped lips, the teeth prominent, almost beautiful, the eyes half veiled and blind, the tits dried to empty triangular dugs; the child, foetus-like, weirdly old, an aged embryo, new-born, famished, ancient in the unspoken, unchanging wisdom of suffering, mouth open for food. But there was no food; it was too late for food. She had watched them die: six rolls of Tri-X and four rolls of Agfa. Newsmagazine covers in five countries.

She closed her eyes.

There was no moral complexity in all of this, because there was no alternative. What was, was. What is, is. What shall be, shall be. So be it. Forever and ever. Amen. It was the New World Order.

She opened her eyes. The little boy had stirred in his sleep. He was sucking his thumb. She realized her bones were aching and so she stood up and stretched. Once upon a time she too had sucked her thumb.

She leaned back against the wall. She had photographed so many of them, but that day she focused on just those two, the mother and child. She stayed with them until they died; then she photographed the corpses, the way the flies gathered, the crushed glutinous light—and how it changed—on one open eye. The other photographers had shot the fields and fields of dead, but she had remained focused.

She pushed herself away from the wall and walked to

where the door had once been. The moonlight, coming through the gap in the wall, cast a sharp shadow—her shadow, stark against the floor.

The little boy stirred in his sleep, half turned, and murmured, "*Maman.*"

She stood for a moment, uncertain; then she went back, lay down next to him, slid her arm under and around his shoulders and held him. His breathing smelled like a child's breathing, and the dust and freshly shattered stucco smelled like dust and freshly shattered stucco.

It was strange, feeling the warm body and regular breathing against her skin.

The green bananas were now overripe and spotted like a leopard. Peanut butter and bananas in a sandwich made a perfectly balanced nutritional meal. Years ago, a friend had told her that in a café in Paris. "I was in Israel," said her friend, "broke, totally broke, running away from my boyfriend. I lived on peanut butter and bananas. I was in shape but I was sort of delirious. Like I was becoming a mystic. You understand?" Where, she wondered, was her friend now?

With one blade of the Swiss Army knife, she sliced the banana and smeared peanut butter on the dried bread. She narrowed her eyes and watched the little boy. He was standing in the shattered doorframe looking out over the dusty plain. During the night, she had walked out to the edge of the settlement. The wind had risen freakishly for only a few minutes, and columns of white dust like dervishes swirled in the moonlight. She had hugged herself and watched them until they died and there was only an immense calm made of stars and the chalk-white light of the moon. Then she went back to cradle the little boy and feel his warmth against her body. Now, beyond the shattered walls there was nothing but a shimmering flatness.

"*Viens,*" she said.

The little boy came to her. She handed him half a sandwich and she began to chew her half. She touched the dusty crinkled hair and he looked up at her with eyes that were neither sad nor happy.

The sun was hot.

A water tank was suspended on two rusty crossbars and the showerhead was attached to a pipe that seemed to be attached to the tank. That and one corner was all that was left of the house.

She turned the handle and water came out at first in a dribble and then in a healthy, rusty stream. Like rich old piss, she thought, turning the handle off. She remembered, south of Kiev once, a small tributary of the Dnieper: muscular Ukrainian and Russian girls in cheap transparent underwear splashing in the manure-coloured water. She shot them in Tri-X, glossy and naive as they were: transient peasant beauties who would quickly grow thick and grouchy on potatoes and long winters. It seemed a lifetime ago, and it was.

She undressed the little boy and draped his clothes, piece by piece, over a crumbled wall.

"*Reste là. Voilà!*" She stood back slightly and turned the handle until he was soaked. He shivered and held himself, hands between his thighs, bending forward, his skin catching white gleams. She soaped him all over, shampooed his hair. It was very pleasurable, the smooth skin, slippery, soft, warm, and glossily surface-cool-wet under her fingers.

She turned the handle again and couldn't help laughing when he shivered and danced up and down on the old broken tiles. He looked up at her laughter and grinned a wide little-boy grin. It was the first time he had even smiled.

"*Voilà!*" she said. He was sparkling.

Carefully he dressed himself.

The little boy was rubbing his eyes and watching her light a fire. She crouched and concentrated. She looked around for a few twigs, saw a piece of dried board, went over and picked it up.

She didn't see the snake until it struck.

It was brown, with a flat, triangular head, coiled up, then—leaping, its fangs sinking into her leg. She stepped back, stumbled, fell and hit her head on a rocky outcropping, a fragment of wall. She lay still.

The little boy chased the snake, but it was already zigzagging away, then gone. He looked for other snakes, cautiously lifting boards and small stones. The sun glared down, glinted on his black skin. He crouched next to the woman, adjusted her baseball cap, keeping her face in the shade. Night came. No more sun, no more shade. Night.

"Mister?"

"I'm no mister," she said. It was a hag-like cackle, a croak. Was that her voice? She coughed, her mouth filling with spittle. She swallowed it back.

If you spit you expel the evil spirit.

"*Quelle heure est-il?*" she managed.

"*Jour.*" The little boy's voice.

It is day.

She digested that; her mind was moving in a slow, liquid dance, shimmering. She could see nothing: *Am I blind?*

"*Combien de temps?*" she coughed. "I was asleep how long?"

"*Deux jours,*" the little boy said.

With her right hand she felt the air around her, and the ground. She sat up. Still, she saw only a glare, white brightness. Then — a shadow.

"*Parle,*" she said. "Speak to me."

"*Tu criais, tu pleurais. Tu parlais. J'avais peur.*" The shadow shifted, came closer. "You cried and shouted. You spoke. I was afraid."

She closed her eyes and held her head in her hands. The world was invisible. "*N'aie pas peur,*" she said. "Don't be afraid."

"*Non. Je n'ai plus peur.*" She felt his small hand on her shoulder. "No, I'm not afraid any more."

She ran her fingers through her hair, sticky with sweat. She blinked open her eyes. She had the impression things were somewhat clearer, not much, but somewhat. She could see the little boy's head, his shoulders, a darkness hallowed in brilliance.

"*Il y a des gens?*" She tilted her face towards him. "Is there anybody?"

"*Non. Non. Il n'y a que nous.*" His head moved. "Nobody but us."

"I'm blind," she said, in French.

"Blind?"

"Yes."

"It will go away."

"I hope so. Yes. It will go away." She closed her eyes and remembered the dream or hallucination or whatever it was—the poison, perhaps, had created it. She was very old and blind, a beggar, wandering in a sort of desert, in some archaic land. She felt it all, but she could see nothing—just feel the heat and hear the voices, mocking, scurrilous, pitying voices…

"Let me sleep," she said.

"Yes," said the little boy. "Nothing will happen. I am here."

Eyes closed, tented in her own sweaty darkness, under the shimmering heat, she thought of the little boy. He had had a family, a mother who had loved him, cared for him, a father who was probably rich, certainly powerful, most likely one of the army thugs. They probably lived in a house with a long veranda, slender wooden columns, colonial architecture, white and gracious, with large, high-ceilinged, empty rooms and the blue light of day filtering through the windows. Certainly not like that at all. No, no, no...not like that at all. Perhaps low stucco and geometric, more like Italian colonial than French colonial, like those squared-off little towns de Chirico painted...No...and her mind wandered somewhere else...

In the beginning, there were no stories.

Strange thoughts migrated through her head, phrases that made no sense.

Here is my song, let it sing. It comes from nowhere. It comes from infinity. It comes from me.

When she woke up she was thirsty. Her eyes were a little bit clearer. Not much, but a little bit. Around the sun she could see the brightness, not the sun itself, an immense halo and a series of rainbows.

"Water," she said.

"Water?"

"Yes. Please."

She drank the water and her throat felt smoother; her voice was easier. She sat up. Things would get better soon, she was sure.

"You are Adam," she said, "the first man. I shall call you Adam."

"Adam?" he echoed from the luminous darkness, from her blindness.

She reached out and held him. He leaned against her, pulled close and held her tight.

The next day her eyes cleared, and they started driving towards the capital. They arrived after twenty-four hours on the road.

Everywhere were scenes of panic. Gunfire. The rebel army was approaching.

People fleeing.

Her office had been ransacked. The boy stood in a corner while she fumbled in the shattered drawers for the documents. Ah, yes, no one had discovered them: her husband, now dead...a young son...French citizens...She glanced at the passport photograph. Yes, yes, perhaps it would do.

She went straight to the airport. A French military plane, on the runway, was about to take off.

"*Oui, madame, mais vite, vite.*" The soldier pushed her and the boy through the swinging glass doors.

Shielding Adam with her body, her camera and film on her shoulder, she ran for the aircraft. She looked back; the soldiers were fighting to contain the crowd.

Shots rang out.

She buckled Adam into a seat, stood in the aisle beside him.

"*C'est la révolution,*" said an African businessman standing beside her, wiping his brow. "*C'est la révolution.*"

"*Oui, c'est la révolution,*" she said.

Beyond the tip of the wing, she could see puffs of white smoke. Closer by, buildings were burning, black smoke pouring from balconies. Artillery and mortar shells were already falling near the airport. Soon the runway would be closed, soon there would be nowhere for anyone to escape.

The plane lumbered into position.

Minutes passed. The rebels were already shelling the end of the runway.

"*On négocie,*" said the pilot. "We're negotiating."

Bursts of machine-gun fire, muffled by the sound of the engines.

Then the plane rolled down the runway, accelerating, accelerating, and finally took off, slowly banking up into the blue sky.

Paris in spring. The newly planted trees on the Champs Élysées are in flower.

Laughter from the terrace. Close to the bougainvillaea. Beyond, you can see the Eiffel Tower.

The photographs, and the story, had made her, briefly, once more, an international celebrity.

Today she has invited Nicole and her ten-year-old daughter, a tiny and beautiful blonde, over for tea. As she stands in the kitchen, the water just beginning to boil, she hears more laughter from the terrace. She smiles. She looks out the big window over the sink.

The radio that morning, as she was drinking her first coffee, had reported that the death toll of the civil war was now thought to be between 500,000 and a million; no one knew for sure. She looks up at the neatly aligned boxes — Earl Grey? China Black? English Breakfast?

"Nicole?"

"*Oui?*"

"*Est-ce que tu préfères — ?*"

More laughter from the terrace. She looks out the window and smiles. Adam, turning a somersault, has just made a new friend.

Lollipop

"LOLLIPOP."

Is this my first bottle or my third?

I pour myself another glass.

In the sun the white wine looks yellow.

Over the sea, the sky is so bright, so blue it seems almost black. When you blink, the blue is ripe with menace, pregnant, about to rupture the azure of the afternoon. Soon it will break: an invisible storm upon the shore.

February—and hot as August. I slip on my dark Polaroids.

On the shimmering beach, the girl in the string bikini dances. Her feet shuffle in the sand.

"She wants me to teach her 'Lollipop,'" says Niki. Niki lifts her glass, holds the edge against her prune-dark lips.

Much of the summer, Niki walks around naked, or almost naked. Early in June, her skin is deep amber. At the end of August, it has melted into the colour of molten tar. In the brightness, her skin glimmers, catches the light, drowns the eyes. I could go blind looking at Niki. At night, in midsummer, she's invisible, except for her smile. One August afternoon she squatted naked in a dark country pissoir and, while peeing, invited me in. I couldn't see anything but her smile: bright teeth floating in black. "Ha, ha," she said, "can't see me now!"

Now it's February. She's a midwinter shade of milk chocolate—pale and creamy, almost white.

"Lollipop?"

"You know." Niki begins to sing.

"Really?"

"Yeah. *Really*." In one swallow Niki empties her glass. She picks up a bottle by the neck, holds it sideways and empties it to the last drop. Niki is wearing a flowered bra. It has little pink flowers with pale green leaves floating on a creamy background. Some time ago, after the third bottle—or the fourth—she suddenly unbuttoned and lifted off her blouse, stood up, stretched, and stripped down to jeans and bra. How long ago? I don't know—maybe half an hour. Who knows? Time is suspended.

"It's from the fifties." Niki picks a piece of dark tobacco from her lips; she turns her head sideways and squints at the beach. "'Lollipop.' The fifties. I think."

The girl dances, her string bikini almost invisible. Her bare feet shuffle in the sand. Slowly she works her elbows, in and out.

The girl in the string bikini is—what was the fifties word?—*stacked*. Yes, she's stacked, definitely stacked. The lion-like mass of stained-blond hair swings heavily when she moves, swishes down to her waist. Two years ago, in an automobile accident, half her face was torn away by glass. People died. She was driving. If you look at her now, it seems she has two faces; it seems she is two women. One smiles, one frowns. Cut in half, right down the middle.

Her bare feet shuffle in the sand and a fine gold chain glints at one ankle.

Screwing up my eyes against the dancing light, I study her closely. Her bikini is tiny.

Niki sees what I am thinking. "Itsy Bitsy Teenie Weenie Yellow Polka Dot Bikini." She grins as she sings. High, boyish, pure, she has a good voice. I'll bet she once sang in a choir. If she didn't, she should have. Niki never has grown up; she never will. Sometimes I think of her as a ragamuffin, sometimes as a nymph, but mostly as just plain Niki—beautiful, irredeemably beautiful Niki.

A waiter arrives. He uncorks another bottle.

The photographer says, "I'm gonna shoot you two guys, okay?" The photographer speaks slangy English with a French accent.

"Sure," says Niki. She grins. "Shoot me!" she shouts in a mock-hysterical voice, shrill and goofy. "Shoot me!" She stretches up her hands, *I surrender*–style.

The photographer crouches across the table. Her blond hair is greased back, her big-lensed black Leica stares at us, cockeyed, an inch above a plate of black mussels. I can see down the photographer's oiled, sweating cleavage. In the wide lens I see myself, serious, aureoled in light, a shadowy caricature. I adjust my hat and glasses. I see Niki too, silhouetted, luminous, clowning—a puppet without strings.

The flash flashes.

"I'm gonna teach her 'Lollipop,'" Niki says.

The flash flashes.

Niki stands up.

"That's good, that's good," says the photographer. She crouches close to the sand and shoots upward, Niki's head against the sky. "*Bien! Très bien!*"

"That's good! Me against the sky," says Niki, pleased. "You're a master, sister. Like Eisenstein. Like Orson Welles. A classic *contre-plongée*." Niki is a polyglot and she knows her movies.

Again, with one hand the dancing girl in the itsy bitsy teenie weenie bikini shakes out her long blond hair. Like a cascade, it falls below her waist, brushes against the naked cheeks of her ass.

The February sun glitters on the sea.

The photographer scratches her head. She turns to the man next to her. He is the cousin of the king of some rich Arab country. The ex-king. She crouches beside his chair, aims the camera upward. He grins down at her. He sticks out his tongue. Her bright blond hair is very short, greased back, like Elvis. Metallic, it glitters. The flash flashes. She grins. "Good!" says the photographer. "*Très bien.*"

Niki climbs up on her chair. She unbuckles her belt. She gyrates her hips. Slowly, she unzips, peels open and peels off her jeans.

Somebody claps.

Her panties have the same rose petals and leaves as the bra. Reaching out her arms, balancing, Niki climbs onto the table.

At the end of the table a fat man with white stubble and thick, wet lips pursed around his thick cigar shouts, "*Brava! Brava, bambina!*"

Niki spreads her legs. In the middle of the table, she straddles, swaying. Empty bottles stand all around her feet.

She sings, "Lollipop."

The girl in the string bikini stops shuffling. She walks up to our table, a band of white sand on her greased ankles. She looks up at Niki.

The photographer, bent in two, creeps around the end of the table. She has startling blue eyes. She flashes upward. She frames both of them: Niki and the girl in the bikini. The girl in the bikini blinks at her. Her mouth makes an "O." The photographer grins and makes an "O" with her thumb and forefinger. "*Très bien,*" she says.

Niki sings. She shuffles, swaying, among the bottles, not touching a single one. She looks down. "You get it?" she asks.

The girl in the bikini, looking up, nods. She sways and then swings her hips, jiggles her breasts. She begins to shuffle again.

"I'll write it down." Niki climbs down from the table. She picks up a bottle and fills her glass. She looks over at me, lowering her chin, tilting her amber eyes from behind the dark glasses, and grins.

The photographer reaches for more film. She plunges her hand into her tan chamois jacket. It's got lots of pockets. Her tan chamois pants are like a second skin. Her black glasses are tilted up on her hair. She pulls them down. She disappears—now she's just cheekbones and full lips. The lips smile. There is a small gap between her two front teeth. "Gotta reload," she says. Swaying slightly, she walks to the men's washroom—it's pitch black and smells heavily of turpentine, fresh piss and wet sand on concrete.

In a high-pitched voice, the girl in the string bikini says, "I'll bet I can sing 'Lollipop.'" Nervously, she clears her throat, looks at her toes, shuffles.

The photographer comes back and sits down next to the Cousin of the King. He squints, trying to see inside her dark glasses. "I used to be a model, once," she says. The Cousin of the King nods, stares. The photographer fills her glass. "Years ago."

"A model." Noncommittal, the Cousin of the King smiles. He has large teeth, a full belly under his T-shirt, a droopy mustache, and an unkempt black beard. He looks like a famous Italo-American film director. His ambition is to look like a famous Italo-American film director.

The photographer holds the bottle sideways, fills Cousin of the King's glass. "In New York. Paris too," she says.

"New York," he says, "Paris." There is a hint of throaty nostalgia in his voice, just a hint. He clears his throat. He squints at the photographer. He would like to see her eyes. But for now her cheekbones and lips must suffice. She has a nice chin. Her neck is long and gracious. It's clear the Cousin of the King likes the way the photographer cuts her hair, like a boy—short, virile, slicked back. Her skin, like her hair, is gold.

"I can sing 'Lollipop,'" says the girl in the bikini. One side of the bikini top has slipped. It shows a wide, dark areola and part of a nipple. I glance at Niki. Niki glances at me. She tilts her head. Over the top of her glasses she winks slowly. We both hope the rest of the top will fall away.

The girl starts to sing. She has a high voice. A child's voice. It breaks easily. Suddenly I feel sad.

"I bet you don't remember it!" shouts Niki. Her voice breaks into the afternoon. Her skin is already darker. Like a blotter she absorbs the sun and sea air. She reminds me of Little Black Sambo and I know I am once again in love.

"Huh?" says the girl in the bikini.

"Bet you don't remember," says Niki.

"I'll remember," says the girl. For a big, voluptuous girl, she has a tiny voice. Shyly, timidly, she smiles. The scarred half of her face can't smile. It's like a mask. She is comedy and tragedy, all in one.

"Bet you don't." Niki stands up and walks over to her. Niki looks mean, pugnacious, her fists are curled, her thin biceps stand out. I know she's raring to fight. I would like to see that. I turn sideways in my chair to watch.

"She's drunk," says the photographer. She turns in her chair too.

"That's all right," says the Cousin of the King.

The photographer puts her arm over his shoulder. I can see the Cousin of the King enjoying the weight of her arm, the touch of this woman he has never seen before. Her open jacket hangs away. Her breasts stretch the thin black T-shirt. No bra. How nice, I think, looking carefully. The Cousin of the King sees me and he thinks the same thing. One of his thick-lidded eyes closes in a lazy half wink.

"If I don't remember it, I'll..." The girl in the itsy bitsy teenie weenie bikini looks as though she's going to cry. Her tragic side is turned to me. "I'll..." She looks around.

"If you don't remember, you'll go for a swim," says Niki. She laughs, *Hee, hee, hee.* And I think, not for the first time, how strange it is; she has an old man's way of laughing, an old black man's wheeze, *Hee, hee, hee, hee,* high-pitched and breathless.

Against the light, I can hardly see her. I want to put my arms around her, run my fingers down her spine. She's a thin bundle, nervous, slender muscle, quick and dignified, even when drunk. She's darker now. Developed by the light like a quick negative. The sun glances off her body. Cool anthracite. The flowers and leaves on the pale panties and bra seem to blink. "You'll go in the water over your head," says Niki. "And you'll drink a whole bottle of white wine. *Hee, hee, hee.*"

"I drink the wine," says the girl, repeating carefully. "The whole bottle."

"Do you think she'll remember?" the photographer asks me.

"I dunno."

"That water's pretty cold." The photographer shivers. She leans closer on the Cousin of the King. He smiles, raises his bushy eyebrows, winks and reaches for his glass.

We look at the water. It's a flat blue oily surface with a lazy swell, slowly breathing. Far out, sketched on the horizon, is the faded blue silhouette of an oil tanker.

The girl sings.

After a few words, her voice breaks. She forgets her lines.

Everybody looks at her. Even Niki is serious.

"I wanted to take a swim anyway," says the girl. Her smiling side is turned towards me. She is beautiful. A profile I will dream about.

I wonder how old she is, twenty-seven, twenty-eight? Or maybe she's younger. The body is ripe, overripe. The scars on her face make it hard to tell.

"I told you." Niki sits down, puts her elbows on the table, empties her glass, pours herself another. "I'll copy it out for her." She drinks. "She'll never remember anything anyway." The sun gleams on Niki's shoulders. She is all smooth muscle. Idly I muse about why I like small muscular black women and why I like slender blondes with French accents and their hair cut short like a boy's. Or overripe childish women with . . . I pour myself another glass.

The photographer and the Cousin of the King turn back to face the table, but the photographer leaves her left arm slung around the Cousin of the King's shoulders.

"I like to drink," says the photographer.

"*Hee, hee, hee,*" wheezes Niki. She clinks her glass against the photographer's and then against the Cousin of the King's and then against mine. "We *all* like to drink," she says.

The girl with the scarred face sings the first lines of "Lollipop." She stops and shakes out her long blond hair. No one is looking. No one is listening. She turns away and starts walking down to the shore. From behind the Polaroids my eyes follow her. It is a slow, lazy, swaying walk she has. The beach and the horizon are absolutely flat. The oil tanker is just a shadow. The string of the bikini bottom disappears into the crack of the girl's ass. She looks naked. There is nothing there but her—her, the sea, and the sky. She looks like the world had just been invented, just for her.

I don't hear a sound. Perhaps I have suddenly gone deaf.

The sky is heavy with blue, blinding blue. I blink.

"We all like to drink! Ha! Speak for yourself!" shouts the fat man at the end of the table. He grins and raises a glass of vodka. His teeth are bad, and sun glints on his heavy, blotched, unshaven cheeks. "*Saludo!*" he says and downs the glass. He picks up the vodka bottle for a refill.

Down on the beach the girl in the bikini now stands at the edge of the water.

She is a small silhouette against the light.

We all look at her.

We all imagine the winter-cold water lapping at her toes. We all raise our glasses and drink.

"She's not going in," says Niki. She squints towards the sea. She leans forward, elbows on thighs. She looks like a little girl in her flowery bra and panties, or like a little boy about to start a fight. I pour myself another glass. If I drink enough maybe I'll discover all about all of this. If I drink enough I'll forget what I discover. I wonder if drink is cheaper than psychoanalysis. It surely is.

The photographer leans her head on the Cousin of the King's shoulder. The Cousin of the King takes a deep breath and smiles. The air is sweet with ozone. The photographer's hair, I imagine, smells like shampoo and sunshine. Niki's hair smells like rich dark spices from some imaginary Orient. Niki's hair smells like night, not like day. "I'll bet she does," says the photographer. "I'll bet she goes in."

"How much?" Niki grins.

"You go in too." The photographer smiles.

"Huh?"

"You lose, you swim. Over your head."

Niki makes a pouty grimace. "No way! That water is filthy!"

I can see the Cousin of the King thinks it is very fine sitting in the hot winter sun with the photographer's arm lying on his shoulder and with Niki sitting across from him in a flowered bra. The photographer's fingers are massaging the Cousin of the King's shoulder muscles. The Cousin of the King half closes his eyes and rolls his shoulders—a pleased tomcat. The photographer shows her teeth in a smile. Niki is hunched over, squinting at the Lollipop girl. The oily glare off the sea makes it impossible to focus. The Lollipop girl is the size of a tiny doll, standing with her back to us, knee-deep in the still water.

"Go girl! Go!" shouts the fat man from the end of the table. He stands up unsteadily, pours more vodka into his glass, squints at the girl on the beach and then sits down. The woman with him—a gaunt Italian brunette, tanned walnut-brown—reaches over, smoothes down his spiky hair.

I think maybe the Lollipop girl is freezing and has just stopped, frozen stiff, her blood turned to ice. The water in February is cold. Or maybe she is scared. Or maybe she's just standing in the sea, ankle-deep, with her back to the land: nothing in front of her but the light and the water, her mind emptied out, stuck in eternity. I lift my glass and drink it empty.

"I think she will," says the photographer.

"You're full of shit," says Niki and grins at the photographer. It's a cocky, crooked grin, a fighter's grin. I think maybe I should get a copy of *Little Black Sambo* and figure out why Niki reminds me of Little Black Sambo. I don't remember anything about Little Black Sambo.

Lollipop is now knee-deep in the water.

"She's going very slowly," says the photographer. She leans back against the Cousin of the King.

"She hasn't got the guts," says Niki, leaning forward like

a sports fan watching TV. She looks the photographer in the eye. "You wanna wrestle?" she says.

"Wrestle?"

"Don't do it," says the Cousin of the King. "She's dangerous. See the muscles."

"No. Not now." The photographer, her head still posed lightly on the Cousin of the King's shoulder, holds Niki's stare from behind her dark glasses. "I can photograph you nude if you want," she says.

"Nude? No. Not now." Niki grins from behind her glasses. She turns to look at the girl in the bikini. "Look. She hasn't moved."

"We can bet," says the photographer. Her long fingers move on the Cousin of the King's shoulders. "If she goes in, I photograph you nude on the beach in the sun—and there, in the shadow of that boat." She motions with her chin towards a large wooden fishing boat, lying tipped on its side. The white paint of the hull, dry and flaking, looks thick and creamy. I think of a painting. A Cézanne, perhaps, walls in Upper Provence in the winter sun, or an abstract surface by Borduas, vibrant, deep, and peaceful. I think of the quiddity of substance, the inescapable tangibility of now, the irredeemable nature of time; I think of stasis and movement, of how each instant is unique, of how each instant is eternal. I think of time and of place, of how eons and infinities, at least 14 billion years and God knows how much space, have intersected just here, just now, to give us, for an instant that may be briefly remembered but that will never again return, this moment: Niki, the photographer, the Cousin of the King, the Lollipop girl, the oil tanker hanging like a shadow on the horizon. *Ah, qu'on était jeune, une fois!* I'm drunk.

The photographer smiles, a lazy, predatory smile. Her big eyes hide behind the glasses.

Niki doesn't turn around. She is thinking. I am thinking too. I hope she accepts. A nude photograph of Niki would be something. Seeing her strut around on the beach naked in February would be something. Seeing her and the photographer together would be something. If they wrestled it would be something. Really something. I empty my glass.

"No," says Niki softly. "Not now." Without looking she reaches back for her glass. I realize Niki is excited; she is tempted, but I know she's not going to do it.

"It's nice here," says the photographer, relaxing, her head lolled back on the shoulder of the Cousin of the King.

The Lollipop girl is in the water, up to her thighs.

Without looking back at the beach, she slips off her bikini top and steps out of her bikini bottom and stands, naked, looking at the blue horizon. The oil tanker hangs high in the sky.

Nobody notices that the Lollipop girl is naked.

Only me.

Lollipop doesn't notice that nobody has noticed. Without turning around she tosses the crumpled bikini underhand onto the beach.

I remember all the times I've spent with Niki. I think about how much we have drunk. *Boy!* Behind my Polaroids I blink. The white flaky paint of the ribbed upturned boat is real, chalky and smooth. More *real* than anything has ever been real, more *present* than anything has ever been — to me. Such mystical moments come after the third bottle.

"See!" says the photographer.

"Well, I'll be fried." Niki stands up. She shields her eyes with one hand. It looks like she's saluting the sea.

Lollipop has taken the plunge.

We all watch.

Even the ripples are invisible. The glare of the low sun has turned the water into molten gold.

The fat man at the end of the table stands up and shouts *"Brava!"* He picks up the bottle of vodka, holds it by the neck and drinks. The gaunt, elegant woman beside him smiles. The squid-ink in the spaghetti has turned her lips black.

"She won't drown, will she?"

"The water's too shallow," says the fat man. Vodka dribbles on his stubbled chin; it blinks back the light. His cheeks are puffy. He's working at it; he's determined to die soon.

"I'm going to shoot her," says the photographer. She disengages from the Cousin of the King, ruffling his hair as she stands. She picks up the Leica.

Steadying myself against my chair, I stand up too. I follow her.

We walk barefoot across the beach.

The sand is crisp, hot on top, clammy cold underneath. A thin crust away from winter. My toes, the soles of my feet, break through. I think of the cold winter sun, of the storms, of the rollers in winter blizzards, of grey skies, of ice spray breaking against the restaurant windows. On winter nights Angelo grills the fish inside and our wool clothes smell of smoke.

"Maybe she will be famous someday," says the photographer, carefully pronouncing the English words. "Lollipop. Then I have her picture. I have the rights. I have everything." In midstride the photographer turns, smiles. From behind her glasses she asks, "That girl has been hurt bad. How did it happen?"

"A car crash, I think. She went through the windshield. Smashed against a tree. All that glass."

"Ah." The photographer nods. It is enough. She squints at the brilliance of the water.

The girl is swimming now, not far from shore.

The photographer stops. "Hold this," she says. She hands me the Leica. She unzips and peels off the skin-tight chamois trousers. Underneath she's wearing slick black panties. Her legs are long, tanned like her face. She hands me the pants, takes off her dark glasses and lays them in my hand. "Thanks," she says, her face suddenly naked. "*Merci.*" She squints out to sea.

The naked girl with the scarred face has come to a shallow bank of sand. She stands up, slowly rising out of the water. The water drips, the sunlight runs off her in rivulets.

I shade my eyes. She shakes herself. Spray. Her blond hair is plastered down thick, coated to her back.

Carefully, the photographer wades into the water.

In a trembling voice the girl sings.

The photographer wades out to the sandbank. She starts to shoot the girl. She shoots her from below, from the side, against the light, with the light.

The girl at first doesn't seem to know she's there. She stands, legs slightly apart, and sings.

I hold the photographer's pants and dark glasses and I look up and down the beach. I squint against the light: nobody in sight. It is February. A few gulls swing low, caw, and swing away. The shadow of the oil tanker hangs, suspended in the blue of the sky, floating above the horizon. Unreal.

The photographer takes some last close-ups. She shoots from the left and from the right side. She closes in, angling for shots, closer and closer. She shoots a frontal close-up. Then she stands close to the girl.

The girl's pose has not changed. Ankle-deep on the sandbank, she has begun to dance, elbows close to her side, pumping her arms, shuffling her feet, stirring the shallow, oily, gently rippling water. She sings.

The photographer glances back at me. She looks at the girl. "Come on, honey," she says to the girl, "you won, you made your point, it's cold, come on... *Viens, viens avec moi.*"

Two women suspended in a world of reflections. The photographer reaches out and touches the girl on the shoulder.

The girl keeps singing. But her singing slows down, like a turntable, its batteries dying.

I shield my eyes.

Two women. There they are, suspended in water and air. The girl turns to look at the photographer. The girl's eyes fill with water. She is crying.

The photographer reaches out, touches the tears. Light shimmers up over them. It's hard to look at them now.

"Come on, honey. Let's go." The photographer is shivering. The water is ice cold.

The girl takes the photographer's hand.

They wade back to shore. The girl won't let go of the photographer's hand. She is covered in goosebumps; her skin is turning blue. "I know the song," she says, glancing shyly at me, then at the photographer. One eye doesn't move. She really does have a voluptuous body, I think, and she doesn't know she is naked.

Water drips from her legs. I hand her the rolled-up, sandy bikini. She looks at it and then says "Oh," and starts to pull it on.

The photographer hands me the Leica and takes her sunglasses. She slips them on. Her greased-back hair gleams like metal. She takes her pants, but she doesn't put them on. Her legs are still wet, glimmering with goosebumps.

We walk back across the sand. Our shadows are now in front of us; up at the restaurant, our table, with the others sitting around it, seems like a richly lit stage set painted gold, patently theatrical, unreal. The girl starts to sing.

At the table the photographer opens her bag, pulls out a box of pills. "This is an upper, this is a downer."

The Cousin of the King peers down at them. "And this one blows you sideways," he says. He grins. The photographer glances at him. She is indulgent. After all, he is the cousin of a king, an ex-king.

"You wanna blow-job?" says Niki. She looks at me, quizzical, solemn. Her glasses are pushed up over her thick Afro. Her face is a dark triangle. The late-afternoon sun spills like pale milk onto her bare shoulders. The flowery bra is immaculate.

Is it two hours later, or three? I don't know. We've pulled the Mini over onto the shoulder of a sandy road a few miles down the beach from the restaurant. A *terrain vague* of weeds and dunes stretches down towards the sea. The windshield is dusty. The sun is bright, already low.

Two boys, coming along the road, toss a ball back and forth. It seems a lazy gesture — soundless and slow.

"You gotta take off your pants," says Niki.

I double up, knees under my chin. My shins bump against the steering wheel. I pull the jeans free. My house keys, looped on the belt, rattle.

"In the back seat, you gotta put 'em."

I throw the jeans in the back seat.

The two boys are coming down the road. They toss a

baseball back and forth. Now I hear their voices, like hollow echoes from another world.

"Your underpants too. You gotta take off."

I slip them off.

"Your T-shirt too."

"Shit. Come on!"

"That's it, baby." She grins. "That's the deal."

"Those kids..."

"Never you mind those kids. Good for their education, they might learn something."

She takes my limp penis in her hand.

"I feel ridiculous."

"*Hee, hee.* You are. You are ridiculous. I wonder what God or whoever was thinking when he made men and women the way we are. The world's ridiculous. Men are ridiculous. You white men are even more ridiculous." She licks her lips and smiles at me slyly.

I am very far away. I squint against the light. She is crouching down. In the smallest space she can curl herself into a tiny ball, a human pretzel.

The two boys come down the road. The ball bounces back and forth between them. The long grass, burnt brown with winter drought, catches the light like white powder.

"It's not very excited." Niki looks up at me, crinkles her forehead.

"Maybe it's the drink," I say.

"Or those pills." She tries again.

"Yeah. Or the pills."

I put my hand on her shoulder. "I'm sorry," I say.

Her eyes are sad. Her face, without her dark glasses, is exposed, a mournful mask.

The two boys cut off the road, head down through the long, slanting grass towards the beach.

Niki tries again. Her hand is soft; her mouth softer. Her tongue is savvy, methodical. I think of her teeth: white, gleaming sharp, moist with saliva.

"I don't think it's gonna work," she says.

"Me neither," I say. I'm a thousand miles away. In memory the flaky white paint of the boat crumbles softly, smoothly, between imagined fingers.

"Let's go to a bar," Niki says. Suddenly she's lively.

"Yeah."

"Drive for a while like that. I like you like that."

"Yeah?"

We drive with me stark naked along the coastal road and come to a bar on a canal where you can sit in a glassed-in terrace and watch the sun go down. We park and I get out and stand naked and barefoot for an instant and then I pull on my bathing suit and then my jeans and T-shirt. Niki stretches, up on tiptoes, arms pointing towards the pale blue afternoon heavens. She twirls around. Slender, muscular—once again she's a little girl. She laughs. This time it's a throaty laugh, a woman's laugh, knowing and smoky and black, a laugh from jazz afternoons and cocktail bars. Slowly she pulls on her jeans, her frilled white blouse, her wide, tightly buckled leather belt, slips into high-heeled sandals. She never wears make-up. Sometimes she will dab on a touch of perfume.

The bar is designed to look like an old-fashioned luxury liner. The waiters all look at us. We are the only customers. We sit far out next to the plate glass, towards the stern, overlooking the sea.

At the table Niki begins to sings softly: "Lollipop."

We drink and watch the sun go down.

"She'll never learn it," says Niki.

"You think so?"

"I know so." Niki takes a long swig. She wipes a glisten of wine from her lips. The candlelight flickers on her skin, dances in her eyes, dark now like tar. "The slivers—the glass—went in her brain. They had to take part of her brain away. Time doesn't go by for her. She's always stuck in the same time, in the same place."

"Forever?"

"Forever and ever and ever." Niki grins. She reaches out, her knuckles brush softly against my lips, back and forth. "I'm starved," she says.

The windows now are sheer black and outside the stars must be up. We are eating lobster and are on our third bottle of wine. The waiter has become very courteous, almost familiar. We are spending money, and though we're very drunk we are polite with a drunken sort of courtliness. It's been a long day's night, as the guy said somewhere back there, in one of those decades we lived through, so fully, so well.

"Remember when I got drunk and destroyed the car?"

"You're drunk now and you destroyed two cars."

"Three."

"Three?"

"That one parked under the trees. Remember? It belonged to that Chinese guy. Boy, was he mad! Remember that time we got lost in the boat?"

"The wind came up." I fill our glasses.

"We were being swept out to sea."

"Yeah. And you kept laughing."

"Yeah! And you kept rowing. Like your life depended on it! Boy, were you mad!"

"Our lives—both of them—did depend on it. The oar kept coming out of the oarlock. Bang, crash, every time I got it in it popped out again. The next island was ten miles away."

"Then...?"

"Then it was open sea. I mean, it was like ocean, we might have starved to death."

"Starved...brrr!" Niki shivers and spears a chunk of lobster.

"Or drowned."

"I hadn't thought of drowning." Niki looks thoughtful.

"It was a distinct possibility. Drowning, I mean." When I begin to hiccup my prose becomes formal.

"Boy, have we done some things. Have we lived! You

remember when you drank so much you carried me on your shoulders all the way home? *Piggy back, piggy back,* all the way home!"

"Yeah, and that cop followed us."

"And you tripped and broke the Chinese vase."

"Uh-huh. It's painful, but I remember"

"That other summer. Remember that French guy on his yacht, the Fascist, Algérie Française and all that. Remember him?

"Yeah. He saw you naked—skin diving, I think—and invited us on board."

"Yeah. His girlfriend, the archaeologist, remember the Bardot pout and how she did a striptease and poured Cognac down her belly?" Niki looks down at her own belly, tugs at her blouse. "And how golden she was?"

"Cognac stings." I don't know why, but in erotic moments I always think of anatomical and epidermic practicalities. I shade the glass of the window and try to see the stars, but all I see is my own reflection and the waiter approaching with another bottle.

"Uh-huh. She wanted in my pants."

I pour us both more wine. "You let her in?"

"No. But I got in hers." Niki casts me the owlish glance; it has the mischievous age-old wisdom of child-like promiscuity. Brief epiphanies. Conquests like trophies in the mind. "Tasted like apples." Niki runs the tip of her tongue along her upper lip.

"The Cognac?"

"Uh-huh. Not just the Cognac. She was a sunny girl."
Niki looks dreamy, palm of her hand against one cheek; she
plays with a dangling lobster claw. "She was all gold, blond
like gold. Smelled like soap and apples."

"Uh-huh." I am jealous of Niki's adventures with
women, though I have my adventures too.

"I love the golden girls," says Niki. She laughs and looks
sideways at the glass where we both see our reflections
reflecting darkly on the stars. "Golden girls are golden," she
says.

There's something metaphysical about all this, but I'm
not sure what it is. I hiccup. I'm at that stage where you
begin to tremble. It will pass.

Orion is up. The wind is warm and brisk, flecked with
invisible spray and salt, ozone rich, smelling of starry
immensities. It is winter after all. Niki leans close to my
arm, presses against me. We bring a blanket from the car.
The car door goes *clunk* in the night. We walk over the
dunes and lie down on the beach and look at the stars. She
tells me stories. Under the blanket our breath is hot. We
pass the bottle back and forth. Cognac, drunk, doesn't sting.
Under the blanket our breath makes us warm.

"Horny?" She's got the giggles—soft, quiet little giggles.

"Horny what?"

"You get horny when you're drunk?" She whispers into
my ear.

"Hangovers."

"Hangovers?"

"Hangovers make me horny."

"Me too. I get the weirdest ideas."

"Yeah. Really weird ways..."

"Fucking. Really weird fucking ways..."

"Me too. I could tell you some things..."

"Me too. I get fucking horny. The things I could do!"

"Tell me some things. Some of the things you could do."

"Molasses on cobblestones. Okay. You're naked, see, and on all fours and the sun is out and you start licking it up and...there's this guy, he's an astronaut and—"

"An astronaut?" I hiccup.

"Yeah."

"In a space suit?"

"He's climbing out of it..."

Much later I tremble and think I'm going to be sick and then I'm calm again. In a low, whispery voice Niki is singing a nursery rhyme. Then Niki is singing some blues tune, sweet and melancholy. Down the beach the lights of the restaurant look like a stranded luxury liner. Then the lights go off and we are alone in the wind.

"I want a twin," Niki whispers. When she says important things, she whispers; she is very shy about important things, even in the middle of the night under a blanket on the beach with just me to hear. Obscenities she likes to shout; love is for whispers.

"A twin?"

"Yeah, I always wanted a twin."

"Girl or boy?"

"Girl. Like me."

"Girl. That's good."

"Exactly like me. Exactly."

"Exactly. That's good."

"I'll look in her eyes and know exactly what she's thinking. And she'll know what I'm thinking. Even when I'm not there. Even when I'm on the other side of the world. Zillions of miles away."

"Uh-huh."

"All the time she'd know everything. Every single thing. I'd never be alone. She'd never be alone. All the time."

"Uh-huh."

"If you have a twin you can share everything."

"That's right. That's very right. Everything. You can share." My hiccups come back.

Orion rises farther, swings around the sky, sinks inland, dissolves away from mind. The wind from the sea is warm for winter, and the night dissolves too, just as the day has dissolved, and the stars.

It is almost dawn when we leave the beach. I stumble once on the sand and I have the tremors again and my teeth chatter and I know I will suffer agony for at least ten hours. I'll be horny. I'll have thoughts. Molasses. Marmalade. Mars Bars. Vaseline. Black binding tape. Whatever. I'll be alone with my horny thoughts. The sun will be too bright. I'll pull down the blinds. In bed I'll lie and sweat alone.

Niki takes my arm. Over the dark dunes and bushes there is one star bright in the milky-bright dawn sky.

Venus, I think. Yes, Venus, the Goddess of Love.

The Champion

"SO — WHAT'S HE CHAMPION OF, ANYWAY?"

"What?"

"He must be champion of something. I mean, if you're champion, you're champion of something, not of nothing, right?" Niki blinks her wide chocolate-and-yellow eyes at me — cat's eyes.

She lifts the soaked sweatband off her forehead; sparkling drops gleam in the gnarled emerald terrycloth. Out of her bag she fishes a new sweatband — it's bone-dry and scarlet. As she leans down, the bright sunlight runs free — liquid silver on her forehead — and suddenly drowns, lost in the black mass of her hair.

Niki's bikini is exactly the shade of her early-summer tan. Later in the season she'll be as dark as anthracite, and the bikini will be coal-black too: invisible at high noon.

"Well, I don't know what he's champion of," I say. "What Mario said was the guy's the champion. Those are his words — 'the champion.'" I hold up the empty bottle, hoping to catch Mario's eye. Crinkling his eyebrows, Mario signals back with a nod of the chin and a knowing grin, one dark gap between his front teeth.

Heat rains down on the tables, vibrates on the corrugated

iron roof of the restaurant and drips on the palm fronds and the bamboo stakes. On the beach, the hot white sand burns the soles of naked feet.

The sky is pure blue, hazy at the edges, darker blue the higher it goes. "Ceramic blue" is what writers call it sometimes—or "celestial blue" is what they say, or "metallic blue"—yes, that's what the sky was yesterday, and the week before, and the week before that. Now the haze has begun, draining the edge out of the blue, making it less "metallic" than it was. It has been pure blue for weeks, maybe months. The sun burns down, blazes off the sea, blazes off everything.

Sitting here is like being branded, enslaved, by the heat. The heat leaves its mark on every bit of skin, on bleached hair, on faded frayed bamboo, on pale denims, and in blue and dark eyes that, after too long in the sun, stare at you fixedly, seemingly empty, seemingly soulless, reflecting nothing but light. Even on black skin, Niki's skin, the heat leaves its darker mark.

"Who is he, anyway?" Niki asks. "That guy, the champion." She motions with her chin.

Mario has just come to our table; he looks back where the champion has just slapped the woman sitting next to him.

It's a hard slap. It echoes. We can hear it from where we sit. Everyone turns, stares, then turns away. A woman at some other table laughs. It's a nervous laugh, quickly subdued.

The slapped woman flinches back, raises her hand to the side of her face.

The champion has a handsome face with blond,

sun-bleached hair, flat, green eyes, a Roman nose smashed sideways, and flesh burned grey and veined red, like a seared steak. Alcohol, they say, will do that to you.

Slouched back in a wooden chair, the champion flashes a winning smile. He seems satisfied with himself. His eyes are far away. He takes a slow, slit-eyed sip of the cheap house white and purses his lips. It's wine the colour of pale piss.

From time to time the champion holds the glass at arm's length and stares at it. His eyes are rimmed red and black like mascara. He looks like a sun- and booze-burnt Peter O'Toole. You can see it: a beautiful young man who has suddenly grown ravaged and old. It has happened so quickly, it's still unreal. It looks as though he's painted on hideous make-up. He's painted a clown's face onto his beauty.

The young woman is still holding the side of her face, eyes wide in shock.

"Fuck," says Niki.

"He's the champion," Mario says, squinting towards the man and uncorking the bottle: prime Tokay. No cheap house piss for Niki.

"Yeah, but what I mean is, what's he champion of, anyway?"

Mario squints. "I don't know." He pulls the cork, smells it and then pours an inch for Niki to test. "I never thought about it."

"You wanna test?" Niki glances at me.

"No, you test."

"I trust the label," says Niki, smiling one of her best smiles up at Mario.

Mario fills two fresh glasses. "If there's a problem, you know where I am." He wipes the neck of the bottle and settles it in the ice in the wine bucket. The ice crackles and sloshes. Mario spins the bottle once and drapes the serviette over it. "Everybody always just calls him the champion. He's been coming since, oh, since last summer, I think. My wife knows all about it. I'll ask my wife. She knows everything." Mario smiles and walks back into the restaurant.

The restaurant is a low, shadowy, two-storey building, set back from the beach. The walls are white stucco, the roof is in red tile, and a corrugated iron overhang covers part of the terrace. Inside the restaurant is a big stone fireplace to grill fish, twenty tables, and a kitchen that can serve a hundred hungry customers at once.

"'My wife, she knows everything,'" says Niki. "Now, ain't that just the way of true love."

"I guess it is."

"Sometimes I wonder about you," says Niki. "You white boys are supposed to be so intelligent..."

"Maybe I got the short end of the gene pool." I study my glass and then gaze at Niki's collarbone. The sun is hitting it at just the right angle: silver running on black, a straight curve, quickly resolved. I sometimes think that every man who really desires a woman becomes, when he looks at her, that woman, for an instant, or just a little part of her.

Mario comes walking across the terrace. It's a weekday

and only about four terrace tables are occupied. He stops at one of the tables, carefully places a tumbler of Amaro Averna next to a lone blonde who is reading *La Stampa* and then comes to us. Shielding his eyes, he glances over at the champion. "Soccer, I think. It was a long time ago. A couple of years at least."

"Fifteen minutes of fame," says Niki when Mario has gone.

"Oh, I don't know. Maybe a year or two."

"Anyway, you can't be a champion of soccer."

"Really? I'm not sure." I raise my glass and look at the light in the white wine. This is fine Tokay: bitter and dry and strong.

"Soccer is a team sport," says Niki. "The way people talk—they don't know what the fuck they mean." She raises her glass, lazily clicks it against mine. "People talk shit most of the time. Even you talk shit. They are very imprecise, people. Language is very imprecise."

"You can say a man is a champion soccer player," I say. "And Italy can sell him for a couple of million dollars to Brazil. That would mean he's a champion, if he's worth that much."

"I don't like it. I don't like the way things slip around." Niki yawns. "The meaning of things is so slippery. It's just like words, to slip around like that." A trickle of sweat dribbles from her collarbone, runs between her breasts. My eyes drift over Niki's skin, over her muscles. I feel the sweaty nervous bundle of skin and muscle under my hands, against my skin, slippery and fleeting, just like words, just like people.

The girl the champion slapped has a Slavic face. Maybe she's a gypsy. Flat face, high, wide cheekbones, big eyes slightly slanted upward and wide apart. Her lips are full and look swollen. She looks like she was a model once, but has since been battered by drinking, by pregnancy—and by love.

She will age badly if she goes on like this, I think.

The eyes look hurt and flat. Stupid—like the eyes of a stunned and uncomprehending animal. They don't see anything; they don't see me.

The champion slaps her again and shouts something. His voice sounds like a bark—raucous, broken. He stands up and bends over her, his face close to her face. He is swearing, I think, but I can't hear the words. The girl looks up at him and then looks away. She doesn't say a word.

"I don't want to watch this," says Niki.

"It's sort of interesting." I pick up my glass.

The girl turns back, wiping her eyes with her knuckles, a naughty kid, ashamed of being punished. Maybe she's retarded, I think, maybe she's simple. The girl's cheeks have red splotches like the cheeks of a clown. Her baby is crying. The girl slips her pareo down, baring a swollen breast, and stuffs the dark, erect nipple into the baby's mouth. Good breasts, I think, the good young, full breasts of a young wet nurse.

"Yuck! I can't stand babies. And a baby screaming!" says

Niki. She stands up. She checks her bikini top, shifts it. I brush some sand from her belly. Her belly is chocolate, flat as a drum, taut. I leave my hand, palm flat, on her hot skin.

"That's my bellybutton you're touching," she says.

"I know."

"Let's go." She blinks at me with a sly smile that's like a child's withheld laughter.

Away from the restaurant awning and the beach umbrellas, the sky is very big. We walk for miles.

The beach is flat and, except for a few towns and cliffs, it goes on for hundreds of miles, broken only by a river mouth or swamp here and there.

The weather shifts, a sudden breeze cuts the sea into diamonds of pure white light.

"I'm going to shave my head," says Niki.

"Oh?" Privately I think this prospect is very interesting.

"Shave my head and wear big round brass earrings, and no clothes. Those slave ones, you know. Like this." With thumb and forefinger Niki shapes the earrings, dangling, enormous brass circles from each earlobe.

"Oh."

"Oh," echoes Niki, drawing it out deadpan. "Oh." She makes a face. "What an asshole!"

We skirt along the dunes, staying close to the foam of the waves. Niki steps into the water and wades along. She shimmers, a dark shadow in the rising glare.

We come to a river. It is shallow and slow and meanders

out across the beach in rivulets like the runoff from some recent storm. On the far side, out in the middle of one of the rivulets, a fisherman is standing. He is fully equipped, with a crumpled cap decorated with fishing flies, and he's wearing boots, trousers, and a bag of gear and is casting a line out into the shallow, sparkling sea.

We start to wade across. The stream is cold and tugs at our ankles and then at our thighs. Niki crosses carefully, with cartoon-like high steps, so as not to disturb the fish or the fisherman. She raises a finger to her lips. "*Shhh!*"

The fisherman turns and looks at us. The sludgy sand shifts under our toes. Niki slips, reaches out for support and squeezes my shoulder, leaving her hand for a moment.

The heat casts a glaze on her shoulders, and white light traces a line along her collarbone and around her belly-button. We wade into the shallows and out of the river. Niki walks up to the man's kit bag. She crouches to look at the man's catch.

"Rain coming in," the man says. He wades out of the river and stands next to us, his boots dripping. He must be fifty, or sixty. It's hard to tell. He hardly looks at Niki. "I got six today," he says, squinting against the burgeoning light. "Storm makes them hungry. Don't know how they sense it."

"Electricity, maybe," says Niki. She straightens up. Now the man looks at her, sees her. Against the rising light, she is an antique statue carved out of black wood: pure ebony.

"Maybe," says the man. He bares his teeth and squints out at the sun, now breaking up into damp shafts of light at the under-edge of a thundercloud. "Or the quality of light," he says. He chews his lower lip, raises the rod and casts again. "Maybe they feel that."

Niki shades her eyes. She follows the direction of his gaze.

"The quality of light," says Niki.

The man reels in and casts again. The line whizzes out, drifting for a moment in a sort of sideways loop, and finally settles down onto the choppy, sparkling water.

Watching the line, Niki puts her hand—still cool from the river—on my shoulder.

Suddenly I think—I don't know why—of a day, years before, when we drove to a mountain village. It was one of those pointless weekend expeditions to nowhere. The village was fortified and gloomy and set high on a hill of dark grey volcanic rock. Niki drove most of the way, then I took over and she slept, waking up to tell me she was having an interesting dream, and then falling asleep again. I never found out what the interesting dream was. She was going to tell me, but then we arrived at the village, and we both forgot. In the village a friend of Niki's had a palazzo, the family castle, which had been empty for years. We could sleep there if we wanted to, so the friend had told Niki.

The watchmen let us into the main apartments, which were ugly, desolate and nondescript, and very old. Through tiny windows cut deep through the fortified walls you could look out over the rolling hills of Tuscany or Umbria or whatever it was. It might even have been Lazio. In the apartments, it was dark and chilly. Outside, the landscape rolled away, field upon field, shimmering and dusty in the hot sun.

Niki looked around the dark rooms. "Ancestral home," she said. "This is a place where people could be really unhappy." She ran her finger down a damasked wall. "I'll bet lots of people died here."

That night, we slept in a big flat, damp bed.

"Love in a lonely place," said Niki. "You know," she turned her face towards me, "I really like the idea of squalor, some kinds of squalor. Like you and me, we could just drink and fuck, and fuck and drink, and live someplace that was no place at all and get drunker and drunker and stupider and stupider and dirtier and dirtier so we'd merge into one person in our dirt and stupor and stupidity. We'd be wrinkled and toothless and bald and we'd drool through our gums as we kissed, both of us. Perfect love! You see what I mean?"

"Maybe."

"*Maybe!* Maybe he sees, and maybe he doesn't! What a prick! What an asshole! You asshole!" Her grin, in the lamplight, was blinding. "You're such a cautious, middle-class white boy. That's really what you are—and I thought the man was a poet!"

She reached out and turned off the light.

The thing was, we didn't fuck at all, Niki and I. Never had and never would. Brother and sister was what we had become, what we were, what we would always be.

In the middle of the night, Niki suddenly sat up in the big flat bed. I woke up slowly, yawned, and groped for the bedside light. Niki was sitting straight up, clutching the thin white sheet to her breasts. "People talk in my head," she said. "People talk in my head too much. They won't shut up." She shook herself, let part of the sheet fall away. "It's one of those nights. Do you ever feel...do you ever feel you're living somebody else's life?"

"What do you mean?"

"It's like playing cards with ghosts. *You deal. No, you deal. No, it's your turn — you deal.*" She was staring straight ahead, not looking at me, not looking at anything, blind to the room. "But the cards have all been dealt before you sit down at the table. You're starting in the middle of the game, and it's always somebody else's game. I'm not even one of the players. I'm just a ghost, an onlooker of my own life."

I slid out of the bed. "Want a glass of water?"

"Yeah. Yeah, thanks." Niki stirred herself, as if waking from a dream, and followed me to the kitchen. "I don't know what the fuck I'm talking about," she said. I poured water from the bottle of Appia into two cloudy glasses. We went to one of the high, narrow French windows. The wind was up and gusts of oven-hot air came in through the open shutters.

We stood in the window, looking at the night.

The landscape was like a ghost landscape, all silvery misty white, rolling away under the invisible moon.

"Those olive trees look like ghosts."

"Yes." Out on the folded hills the olive trees, row upon row, vague like splotches of mist, shimmer and tremble with the shifting light of the moon.

"Remember, my mother is a Voodoo master." Niki turns to me, stares at me from under her eyebrows.

"I remember."

"Just so you don't forget."

"How could I forget?"

"I love you, you know," says Niki.

"Yes, I know."

"And you love me, too," she says.

"Yes, I know. I love you too."

"Love, oh, fateful love," she sings, dancing away from the window, into the shadow, flickers of reflected moonlight pale on her skin.

Perhaps it was the quality of the light seen on that day on the beach or some forgotten configuration of cloud that called up that old memory of that night in the abandoned castle. Perhaps it was the light on Niki's skin, or the way she tilted her head to watch the fisherman cast his line, or the touch of her cool hand on my shoulder.

Suddenly we are in shadow.

The man reels in the empty line.

The heat is gone from our skin.

Niki pulls at her string bottom, readjusts it. The flimsy threads of cloth make her look younger somehow. Naked, she is at once primal and ancient, more innocent and less so, wilder and yet exotically familiar. Clothed, she acquires a reserve, a dignity, which is somehow domestic and almost sombre.

"Electricity," says the man. Again he casts, again he reels in, slowly this time, intently. He's doing it, I think, for Niki. The webbed cap casts a green shadow on his forehead and gold-rimmed tinted glasses. He must be about sixty, I think, now that I see him more clearly. Probably he's a business-man. "They say snakes can tell an earthquake coming by the electricity. But why should there be electricity?" He glances at Niki.

"The pressure in the rocks polarizes the air pockets, changes the electromagnetic field. Something like that," says Niki, narrowing her eyes, following the glittering line as it reels in.

The man's eyes flicker over her body and I don't blame him. Often my eyes flicker over her body or stay put and just stare.

It's as if I am blind when I look at Niki. My hands and body think of her, not my eyes—my eyes are too full, full to overflowing.

The man looks at me and crinkles his eyes. "She knows a lot about it," he says.

"She reads a lot," I say. "She's an encyclopedia."

"I'm just fucking intelligent." She grins. Her hair sparkles, her forehead glows with sweat. In the hot, dry breeze, I catch a whiff of her dark, spicy perfume. She blinks at me, half closing her eyes.

The man kneels and pulls a bottle out of his sack. "This is pretty good grappa. It comes from my part of the country, up north." He cradles the flat bottle in his palm and squints up at the clouds. "Soon it will rain." He holds the bottle out to Niki.

"I don't mind if I do," says Niki. "Thank you." She takes the bottle from the man and gulps down the grappa, making a face. *I don't mind if I do.* Once again I wonder about how and where she learned to talk. She has some beats and rhythms that come from old TV movies, Broadway musicals from the 1940s, hipster talk from the fifties, black talk from Saint Louis and Harlem, Creole French from Haiti. She went to school in Switzerland, lived in Paris and Chicago, spent teenage winters in Haiti, bummed around in Israel, and has lived most of her adult life in Italy. She's one mixed-up polyglot kid, shifting like the iridescence in an opal.

By the time we wade back across the stream we have the man's telephone number and his address. He's originally from the Friuli region, he tells us, but now lives in Rome. He makes his own grappa, he tells us, and he fishes for his own fish and he has a garden full of his own real tomatoes. His wife is a real cook, he tells us, and his oldest daughter is about Niki's age. She's a pediatrician in Milan and very successful. The other kids—three of them—are grown, too, but come out sometimes for weekends, and for years now he and his wife have rented one of the houses in the fishing village, just up stream. In the back yard of the rented house they grow their own tomatoes, tomatoes in rows, and his wife makes sauce for pasta and for polenta out of the very same tomatoes—the tomatoes they grow.

We glance upstream, towards the fishing village. The small stucco houses sit on the edge of the stream, with little boats tied up behind them, and big funnel-shaped nets suspended out over the water, nets you can lower down to catch the fish as they swim up or down the river. It's the sort of simple out-of-the-way place that looks like it has been there for a hundred years. You can imagine yourself living there, in such a place, where everything is simple and the sun is warm and nothing ever changes.

Niki and I shake hands with the fisherman, wave goodbye and begin the long trek back. High over the sea, the clouds darken.

"People think things happen," says Niki. "But nothing ever happens."

"Oh."

"Yes, 'oh.'"

"You are being very difficult today."

"I'm going to grow tomatoes."

"Tomatoes?"

"Yeah, tomatoes with stalks. And in rows."

"I see."

"I'm going to kneel down on the earth, on my knees, in between those rows of tomatoes, and I'm going to tend those stalks. They're going to be the most beautiful tomatoes ever, the most beautiful tomatoes in the whole wide world."

"Next thing, you'll be making tomato sauce."

"That too."

"And having babies."

"Shut up."

"And slipping your nightgown off your shoulder, offering your breasts, dripping warm watery milk, and—"

"Shut up."

Niki takes my hand and we walk for a while in silence. Babies are a sore point with Niki. She always says she doesn't want to have children. And yet, now she has doubts. I guess we all ask the same question. Who am I, now, without anchors, without progeny, without family, without even a tomato plot to call my own?

A first skirmish of hot rain hits us and Niki is suddenly happy. She dances away from me, then circles around, raising her hands up to the rain: a rain dance, a sun dance—*hallelujah*!

As suddenly as it began, the rain stops. Once again the sun shines. Mist rises from the hot sand.

Niki stretches, her arms reach above her head. Without speaking, we walk on.

"You think I'm a girl out of some fucking poem," says Niki. The accusation comes out of nowhere. No—maybe not from nowhere. Maybe it's me. Maybe that's what makes her angry—and amused.

"You *are* a fucking poem."

"Yeah." She laughs. She dances away from me, dangling her arms out like a scarecrow. "I'm a poem! I'm a poem! I'm a fucking poem!"

The wind turns. The blue waves are crisp and dark. As we wade across another small stream, the water suddenly piles up—deeper, darker, driven back inland by the wind.

The sun is gone. Everything is dull, and Niki's skin turns matte.

We finish crossing the little stream and wade out of the water. Why is her smile so beautiful? I take her hand.

"You have a bright smile," I say.

"Don't I, now." Her hand tightens on mine. "We black folk are very bright. We have big white smiles. It's a well-known fact."

Two sun-soaked girls, wet now and gleaming white, stand on the dunes, brushing the sand off.

The heat is heavy but the air feels cool in the sudden shadow.

For a moment, the brightness of summer has retreated far out to sea where the sun still shines and brilliant summer drifts, shimmering on the horizon.

The real rain starts as we get back to the restaurant. Large drops fall on the brown sand; the dark splashes spread. Then the rain drums on the corrugated tin roof.

The champion is leaning back against his chair, his head cocked to one side. It looks like he's asleep, but his eyes are open. The woman is walking up and down in her pareo, bare-foot, cradling the baby and crooning a soft, mournful sound. She walks like a dancer, toes pointed outward with the soles of her feet flat on the ground. Niki watches her come and go.

"You know what love is?"

"No." I'm chewing Greek olives. "No, I don't know. What is love?" I pick the olives one at a time out of the bowl. They're salty and fleshy and sweet with olive oil. They crumble on your tongue. I work the pits free with my tongue and teeth and pick them out of my mouth and plant them in the ashtray in a small pyramid.

"Love is loss."

"Oh."

"Love is hunger."

"Oh."

"Love is anger."

"Oh."

"Love is hate." Niki is staring at the girl carrying the baby. The girl has stopped at the edge of the terrace, where the corrugated roof ends and where the silver slanting rain is pouring down. She is looking out at the rain and the beach and the sea. It looks like autumn, cold and dreary, in spite of the heat. The girl holds the baby tight against the brightly coloured pareo.

I lift another olive out of the bowl, contemplate it for a moment and pop it into my mouth.

Niki is still watching the girl. "You know if you see a bug, say a neat little ant, you look at it for a while, then you put your finger down close to it, and you poke it around, see it run, see it try to escape. 'Hello, little ant,' you say. 'Hello, little ant. Hi, how are you?' The ant of course doesn't answer. Right?"

"Yes, I've done that."

"Then for some reason—you don't know why and you don't really think about it—you use your little finger, maybe your thumb or your index finger, and you crush it. Twist it into the cement. So there's nothing left."

"Yes."

"That's hunger. That's love."

A couple of days later, back in town, Niki and I play at getting drunk. At lunch, we drink three bottles of wine then three glasses of grappa each. We start to grope each other in the restaurant. I slide my fingers down her back, then between her belt and her skin. I move around to her hot smooth belly, the crisp dry pubic hair, the warm curved beginning of her thighs.

Outside the restaurant, after they've closed, I push Niki up against the wooden cart of the local junkman. He's a small, wizened, amiable man in a dark cloth cap and jacket who pushes his cart up and down the streets and rings his bell. It's his day off. The cart is parked, tilted up on its end, beside an ivy-covered burnt-sienna wall. I unbuckle her belt and slide my hands down under her jeans, over her ass. I put my mouth on hers. It's a hot, sunny afternoon and there's nobody in the streets.

Niki's mouth always surprises me. It's so soft, and while we kiss she has a way of staring at me, never closing her eyes, just narrowing them to slits, staring at me from some huge distance, like from another star. The curved cheeks of her backside give me an ache that is difficult to contain. The flat, hard curve of her belly gives me echoes of that ache. In my eyes, her eyes—are they quizzical, arrogant, startled, lustful, amorous, or merely amused? Yes, her eyes give me an ache and I know I will never be cured.

"We're crazy," says Niki.

"Sure, we're crazy," I say.

"Yeah, and people are going to see us."

"I don't care."

"I don't fucking well care," Niki sings. She tilts her head back and bellows, "I don't fucking well care! Hear ye, Hear ye! Come see! I don't fucking well care!"

It is siesta time; the street and square are empty, dozing.

I bring my hands up, start unbuttoning her shirt. "No bra, baby, no bra. Boy, am I liberated! Am I free!" With the tips of my fingers, gingerly, I touch her small, precise breasts, nipples erect, wanting to kiss them, and wanting to kiss her belly, but finding it awkward to bend or to kneel, here, on the cobblestones. Her forehead glows. Already, from the other day's sun, she's smooth and glossy and black, as if coated in oil.

"Are we really crazy?"

"No, we're not crazy at all."

Suddenly we are up in this apartment. I don't remember how we got here, but here we are. Oh, yes, now I remember, we were out there groping, on the piazza, with Niki up on the junkman's cart. I was fondling her, running my hands up her legs, up her thighs, kissing her breasts, when this black woman—Gloria is her name, a friend of Niki's—comes along.

"You two look like you're having a rare good time."

"Uh...yeah..."

"Come on up and have a drink. Up there," she says, nodding at a row of geraniums, five floors up, on a wrought-iron balcony.

We go in through the big portals of the palazzo and we walk through the entry, over the cool floor, over the speckled white-and-black marble floor. Blurred images of Niki and me flicker in the big gilt-framed mirrors. Then, somehow, we are riding up in the elevator, a cage of wrought iron, slowly rising, until it comes to a sudden, sickening stop, and the door creaks open.

"Home, sweet home," says Gloria. She is a tall, distinguished-looking woman, wearing open-toed leather sandals and lots of gold bangles. When I think back on it, Gloria probably saved us from getting arrested. Even Italy has its limits.

So there we are—Chez Gloria. Outside, the sun is excessively, unbearably bright.

"Well, are we drunk or are we drunk!" I look around. This is a fine apartment. I imagine it in winter, the icy rain falling outside, the fire burning merrily, the curtains pulled shut against the outside, the paintings bright and warm on the walls.

"You shouldn't let him drink so much," says Gloria.

Out on the balcony, beyond the open doors, the geraniums are very bright.

"Those flowers are very bright," I say. "They are too fucking bright."

"You are fucking pissed out of your mind," says Niki. "He's pissed out of his mind."

"I can see that," says Gloria.

"The day is too bright too," I say. "Have you ever noticed how bright the sun is? It's too bright, that's what it is—it's too bright."

Gloria brings a bottle of Cognac. We start smoking, handing the cigarettes around and drinking from oversized snifters. The Cognac makes the day even hotter. The smoke makes it cooler and brighter still. Gloria puts on music. I can see the notes, the individual notes, the timbres, the echoes, the smoky clarinets, the throaty bassoon, the spine-tingling, thrilling violin, I see it all in my mind, feel it in my gut, sublime and silent, like a poem.

Then I'm at home in bed alone and I have a headache.

It must be day. No, maybe it's night. All the shutters are shut, the curtains drawn. I pad around barefoot and naked, the soles of my feet cool on the marble tiles. I push back some curtains. Bars of searing dusty light break through the slates of the shutters. I pull the curtains shut. I decide I am thirsty. I go to the refrigerator and grab a bottle of beer. I pop off the cap and drink. My flesh glows, hot and bright and painful as a phosphorescent fire.

Niki phones and tells me to come out and play and that I can't stay in all day. So we go shopping. I have a hangover and wear dark glasses with white plastic frames, and, for added effect, Niki paints scarlet lipstick on my lips.

"*Slave Girl.* It's new. I think I'll like this one. And *Vamparella.*"

"This one's cool. This mad doctor amputates the girl's arms—"

"Yeah, let's get that one too."

"Here the two beautiful wicked lovers are accidentally burned in a fire they deliberately set to kill his wife, and are made so ugly—so grotesque—that they can't even show their faces outside the—"

"Yeah."

"Here the girl is tattooed all over, so she can't do anything but perform in a—"

"Good, good."

Niki and I collect Italian pornographic comic books. An old woman sells them from her stall; she wraps them in brown paper. "I have some new ones," she says, and points. Behind her stall is a narrow hole in the wall, piled on all sides with *National Geographic*s, Periodic Encyclopedias (*A History of Renaissance Art, A History of Knitting, A History of Soccer*), skin magazines, beaver magazines, and pornographic comic books.

"Yeah, I like this one." Niki flicks the pages. "So while she's unconscious, he gets out his do-it-yourself kit, right, and he pierces her and puts in these rings, welds them shut, you see, so when she wakes up..."

"There's this mad surgeon." I point at the pictures. "And the evil actress thinks she's just gone for a routine bit of plastic surgery, but..."

We discuss what excites us, and why, and we make up stories to fill out the stories that the comic books tell. *Slave Girl* is one of Niki's favourites—a curvaceous black slave escapes from her plantation masters, from pirates, from the wicked Ku Klux Klan, from perverted Unionist generals, from Abraham Lincoln, from monsters from outer space, from whatever. In her adventures, she undergoes every tribulation and humiliation and sexual misuse imaginable, only, at the end of each episode, she manages to reverse her servile position—enslaving the slave drivers, making a slave of her white mistress, chaining up the wicked kidnapper, exposing the newspaper publisher for the fraud he is—and emerge triumphant, wearing a cute dress, or bathing suit, or sarong, or Armani suit, or g-string, or whatever. The end.

We sit on the terrace drinking white wine and reading our comic books.

Niki is wearing a khaki shirt and khaki shorts. Her bare feet, black on top and pale dusty white underneath, are propped up on a stool. "Look at this." She hands me a comic. *"Deep Cut: A Prostitute's Revenge."*

"Golly."

"*Golly?*" says Niki. "*Golly?*"

"Gosh, maybe." I stare at the drawing. I turn it upside down. Turning a penis into a labia is a pretty complicated —

"'Gosh' is better," says Niki. "'Golly' makes me think of Golliwog."

"Which is you."

"Which is me," says Niki, and grins. "You fucking racist. You fucking white supremacist racist pig! I'll bet *you* belong to the Ku Klux Klan."

Niki likes mutilation and transformation; she likes reversals. She likes striptease, stripping herself, and other people, until there is nothing left. All identities fade away. They drop off like old clothes until we are naked, like King Lear on the heath. Sometimes, she says, we have to turn ourselves inside out to find out who we really are. Insiders are turned into outsiders, beauties into monstrosities, studs into eunuchs, sadists into masochists, masters into slaves. Subject becomes object; object becomes subject. "It's all very philosophical, ain't it," she says. Niki is my idol, my totem, my fetish, my friend.

Flash. I photograph Niki.

Flash. I shoot Niki.

Flash. I pose Niki.

The shutter clicks and, Niki, you are imprinted on celluloid. I put you in my album, under celluloid. I show you to my friends. I project you on a wall.

You capture me. The shutter clicks. *You put me under celluloid. You project me . . .*

It's amazing, I think, and I tell Niki this: how biblical all of these sadistic fantasies are, how like Greek tragedy with their reversals, their ironies, their retributions and mutilations.

"Look at Oedipus," says Niki.

"Look at Samson."

"Clipped like you," says Niki. She grins. "Shorn of his manhood."

"That's right." I run my hand over my bald crown: prickly.

"Daphne, I like Daphne." Niki's eyes go dreamy, a gluey elliptical rectangle drifting in her eyes. "Just think, being changed into a laurel tree, your skin changing to bark, your hair to twigs and branches and fluttering green leaves, your feet to roots and tendrils digging deep into the damp dirt. Just think!"

"Or Narcissus."

"Yeah, Narcissus, leaning into the mirror of the pond."

"Becomes a flower."

Niki puts away the book she's been flipping through. "If you look at the Garden of Eden, say, well, when they eat the apple from the tree of knowledge, it's the first time they really *see* each other, you see what I mean."

"Yes."

"I mean, really *see*. It's the other side of blindness. If they hadn't eaten the apple they wouldn't even have known they were fucking when they were fucking, for God's sake! The very idea."

"That's right."

"He's a real trickster, God."

I hold out a comic book. It is a cartoon of complicated bondage, a visual joke, a physical impossibility. "I wonder if the champion would like this."

"He wouldn't understand it."

"Oh?"

"Yeah, 'oh.' If you know this stuff, you know too much about yourself to be stupid like he's stupid, cruel like he's cruel."

"I don't know about that."

"If you know your own monsters, it's harder to become one."

"I'm not sure knowing your own monsters helps. Some people act things out. They actually try to do those things, even if they have read all the books—maybe *because* they've read all the books."

"Maybe. But then they are stupid. There's a big difference between a cartoon and real people. I mean, cats and mice are *not* Tom and Jerry."

"So where's the champion?" says Niki. We haven't been out to the beach in almost a month.

"I haven't seen him," says Mario. "He doesn't come here any more."

"He doesn't?" I feel the world has collapsed.

"Didn't pay his bills." Mario frowns. "About 500,000 lire."

"Fuck!" Niki is truly scandalized.

"That's too bad," I say. "Three hundred bucks!"

"Bastard! Where's he gone?" Niki is extracting a snail from its shell.

"Somewhere down near Ostia, I think. I don't know. I'll ask my wife." Mario heads off to ask his wife. The waves are quiet; the sky is pearl grey, and the sun is grey too—a big vague splash in the sky, but hot, and oppressive.

"'My wife, she knows everything,'" says Niki. "True love. That's true love. Why don't we know true love, eh?"

"I don't know," I say. "Maybe the champion knows true love."

"*Him?*" Thoughtfully, she extracts another snail. "I doubt it."

We decide to go look for the champion.

We look up things on maps, we ask questions and we get a few answers. He'd been seen here, then there, then in this other place. We are detectives, Niki and I: it's a new game.

Finally we find the place where he lived, the place where he'd last been seen.

It is on a side street in Ostia—a lane, really—that runs beside a drainage canal, heading sluggishly down to the sea. The lane smells of fertilizer and dead fish and fuel oil. On the other side of the drainage canal are fields where the sun ripples, a dull white glare, on rows of dusty green corn. Iridescent with white and oily scum, the water hardly moves at all. A large dead fish floats upside down on the surface, its belly white, its gills open, pale rose.

"People end up in the most godawful dead-end places." Niki wrinkles her nose. She squints up and down the lane. "It must be that one over there." She points at a doorway in a low square stucco structure. A number is splashed in black paint near the corner on the grey-blue wall.

"Hello! Hello! Anybody home?"

"I don't think there's anybody—"

The beads in the doorway rattle. They swish apart.

The girl with the flat face has a big dark bruise on her right eye—like a raccoon. As she pushes out between the beads to see who we are, she blinks awkwardly, and I wonder if she is half blind, hostile, or just simple.

"He's not here," she says.

"Where's he gone?" says Niki.

"Come in," says the girl.

As we enter, the beads rattle, and the cool damp in the room suddenly hits us: it smells of sour milk. Flies buzz lazily. The baby is naked and sitting on a wooden table in a puddle of stale milk. Breadcrumbs are soaking up the milk. A soiled diaper lolls on a chair.

"I don't care where he is," says the girl. "I saw you often at Mario's. You were watching. Everybody was watching. Do you want coffee? I can make instant."

"Instant's fine," says Niki.

"Sure, instant's good," I say.

"He's a bad man. He's no fucking good," says the girl. She lifts the kettle onto the stove, lights the gas with a match and stands back. "Most of the people who come here come here to get money. He owes everybody."

"You're better off without him," says Niki. She looks around the room. So this is love, so this is squalor. It is filthy. Pages from old newspapers are scattered on the floor. Men's underpants lie crumpled on one chair, stained bright yellow with urine. The breeze rattles the bead curtain and carries in the dank smell of the drainage canal. Outside, the heat shimmers, blinds the eyes. I turn away and look at the baby. The flies buzz around the baby, landing on its arms, at the corners of its eyes, on the stale pool of milk.

"He'll be back," says the girl. "He always comes back."

The girl shows us newspaper clippings. She keeps them in a brown envelope in her suitcase. Niki glances at each clipping, grunts, and hands them to me. Yes, he was briefly a champion. There are headlines in the sports papers, and big front-page pictures. He is photographed with starlets and millionaires and politicians. I push the papers away: the champion was really somebody, I think. Once upon a time, he was really somebody: he had fame, money, and girls. And he was young too. I stand up and start to pace the room.

The girl talks; Niki listens; I watch. Somehow it's as if I'm outside the room, far from the buzzing flies, the smell of sour milk, the bluish air and soiled diapers. Now I remember seeing the girl, maybe three or four years ago, on a magazine cover, and I remember thinking how beautiful, how desirable, she was. She too was famous, in a way.

Her suitcase is always ready, the girl says. She's from Yugoslavia and came to Italy to work as a model. Then she met the champion.

"It was a mistake. I was on two magazine covers before I met him, good magazines too. The first night, we make love, it is too good, I think, I know it is a mistake. I know it is a mistake, the first night."

"A mistake?" Niki is sitting on the wooden chair, elbows on her knees, leaning forward.

"I am too hungry, I tell myself. I am too hungry for love. It is too violent, I say to myself, it is too good. I say to myself, Yelena, you are a foolish girl."

"Foolish?" says Niki.

The girl looks at her but goes on talking. She is talking to herself, really, not to us. "I say to myself, it is too late, you are too foolish to go back on this. Now you will only go forward. In your belly you will carry his baby, you will have his baby, you will give milk to his baby. When he hits me, I say it is because he is weak, it is because he needs you, it is because he loves you. I tell myself lies, simple lies, and I like telling lies when he hits me. I like to look at the bruises — I touch them — in the mirror. Oh, yes, I think. Look at that, Yelena. Look at how much he loves you. Go out into the street, Yelena. Walk barefoot and buy the vegetables, and show the bruises and the big belly so people can see how much he loves you, how he fucks you, how he hits you: show them how much you are loved."

"So you think that's love," says Niki.

"No, he doesn't love me. I know it now."

"Now you know it," says Niki.

"He likes to fuck me, and hit me."

"Fucking and hitting," says Niki.

"Fucking and hitting, it is the same thing—for him." The girl drinks from the edge of her cup. Her eyes look sly. I drink too. The instant coffee is not at all bad, I think, emptying the cup.

We drank the last of our coffee and said goodbye to the ex-model and went out into the watery hot sunshine. The breeze had disappeared. It was muggy and the air wasn't moving in the alleyway along the edge of the canal. The dead fish was still floating upside down, displaying its white belly and its pink gills. A few leaves, yellow and curled, were drifting in the thick white scum.

Without saying anything we got into the car. I turned on the radio and we got an Italian song—something about what sailors do when they are all alone on ships without any women to comfort them. I put the car in gear, and we pulled out of the lane and onto a local road, paved with old black asphalt, ragged and gravelly at the edges; along part of the road stood a line of tall, dusty poplars. The windows were rolled down and it was like we were sailing through a murky sea.

We drove down to a bar that gave onto the beach.

The sky by this time was white and featureless. The sun had disappeared. Niki sat on a low wall separating the bar from the beach. She played with the opening of her shirt, trying to let in some air.

"Shit," she said.

"Yes."

"Fuck."

"Yes."

"Fuck."

A few weeks later we hear that the champion had been in the corner bar, in that same alleyway in Ostia, drunk one night. They'd had to ask him to leave, which he did. He didn't make a fuss, they said, he just went quietly.

Mario's wife knows all about it. The champion moved on again, she says. The girl came back to the city. She cleaned up her act, got a few modelling jobs. Then she disappeared. "There are Yugoslav gangs," says Mario's wife. "They're pretty tough. You never know what can happen."

"White slave trade," says Niki.

"That's it," says Mario's wife.

The champion, somebody tells us, got a job in a shipyard. Well, it wasn't really a shipyard; it was just a little repair shop where they hoisted small boats on a crane up out of the water to be repaired. "His job was to scrape the old paint off," says one of the workmen. "See that one there. That's the sort of job it needs. That's what he did. It didn't last long, though."

The workman takes us through the shop.

Niki runs her hand over the varnish.

"That's good work. That's smooth," says the workman.

A few days later somebody tells us they heard the champion was selling balloons from a little wooden stand on the nudist beach south of Ostia. So one empty afternoon, Niki and I go to the beach.

"What the hell do they want with balloons on a nudist beach?" says Niki.

—"I have no idea."

—"Volleyball with balloons?"

"For the kids, maybe."

We pull the car over onto the shoulder of the coastal road. Along the narrow road cars are lined up on the shoulders. The pines and cedars of the forest are pale with heat and sun, and the bushes are coated in fine white dust. The sun glints off all the hot roofs and hoods and windshields. The place smells of cedar and resin and of salt and the sea. A few people are standing beside their cars, taking off their clothes.

"When are you going to beat me?" says Niki.

"Beat you?"

"Beat me up. It would be real love, you know." She reaches out so I can help her down the side of a sand dune. The sand slides under her feet.

"I don't think I'll beat you up."
"Black and blue all over. The true sign of love."

The balloon stand wasn't there any more. There was just a faded, crooked sign on a tall wooden pole stuck in the sand that said "Balloons, Candy Bars."

None of the naked people knew anything about it. We asked.

Niki wanted to keep on asking. She liked seeing naked people. So we walked along the beach asking all these naked people about the balloon stand and the guy that had been selling balloons.

One girl, who was sitting alone at the edge of the water, thought she remembered him. "Good looking, burnt-out guy, right?" The girl shaded her eyes, looking up. She unfolded her legs and stood up. She was just the same height as Niki. "Yeah, I saw him, but I never spoke to him. It was like he was on another planet. He had these eyes. I couldn't look into them. They were—how can I say it?—they were empty. There was nobody in there, nobody home." She laughed. "I think he was drunk. I think he was drunk all the time."

We went back to Mario's beach-side restaurant to consider things. A big fire was burning in the fireplace, and Mario's father—a handsome, thickset man with a white handlebar mustache—was grilling fish over the open fire. The room was warm and smelled of wood smoke and frying fish. The windows were steamy, and, beyond them, we could just make out the terrace. The sea was wild, with grey waves and splashes of foam. It looked like a regular ocean.

We sat down near the fire.

On the walls were rows of fading black-and-white publicity photographs of celebrities who had eaten here or drunk out on the terrace or down on the beach in the deck chairs that belonged to the restaurant.

"To the champion."

"To the champion."

"I think in the end he was a failure. That's what did it."

"Everybody's a failure, in the end," said Niki. She nodded towards the photographs. "Look at them—they're all dead."

Two weeks later, I saw Niki off at the airport. She was going back to Paris. We embraced, we held each other and we kissed. Niki—and it was very unusual—was dressed like a woman, with a long skirt, a white blouse, a jacket.

"You'd think we were lovers," she said.

"We *are* lovers," I said.

"Yeah." She considered it for a moment. "I guess in a sense we are."

I watched Niki go through passport control and then, a little farther away, through the security check. She turned and waved. I waved back. Then there were more people in the way: a woman with a baby carriage, and another woman in a sari, and then a group of tourists heavy with cameras and shoulder bags. I couldn't see Niki, so I stood watching for a moment, and when all the people were gone, Niki was gone too.

I went back out to the restaurant on the beach. I walked up and down and looked at the autographed pictures of former patrons. The champion's picture was there too, in a place of honour.

"They're all dead," I said to Mario. "Or almost all."

"Yes."

"So why don't you take the pictures down?"

"I don't like to take the pictures down."

"Why?"

"Well..."

"You're sentimental, I guess," I said.

"Maybe."

"You haven't got a picture of me up there."

Mario grinned and pulled the cork out of the bottle. He poured me a full glass of wine. "You haven't earned it yet."

When Mario had gone back to his cooking, I twirled the glass in my hand and reflected: I often thought of the champion. I found the idea of the champion intriguing, and somehow consoling. Somewhere he's getting drunk, maybe, somewhere he's trying to beat up some woman. Maybe, somewhere, he's lying in a small graveyard near the sea.

I finish my wine and walk down the alleyway beside the restaurant and out onto the beach. There is a chill in the air and it is dark. I can see the lights of a few fishing smacks far out on the sea, and I can see the lights of one of the villages up the coast, the village Niki and I walked to the day we first asked Mario about the champion.

I wonder where the fisherman is now.

I wonder where Niki is now.

Without a moon, all the stars are bright in the sky. I don't know why but it has always comforted me—the thought that those stars were there, in more or less those patterns, when Jesus Christ walked in Galilee, when Mohammed entered Mecca, when Socrates argued about love and seduced beautiful boys in the back alleys of Athens, and when there were no people—no people anywhere at all.

I look up and down the beach and I wonder if the champion is somewhere close to the water looking up at the night sky and if in his eyes he is able to behold eternity and all the love that lies scattered in the stars.

I lie down, flat on my back, on the cold, damp sand and stare straight up. The stars make dizzying patterns, eternally deep.

I half close my eyes. I'm almost falling asleep. I think for a moment of the champion and I open my eyes. The cold breeze suddenly makes my eyes run.

I blink away my tears. The night sky is an infinite assemblage of stars, towering up into depths never yet explored and I feel myself spinning around and around, and sinking, slowly sinking, into that cold dark eternity.

Bevete del Vino

SHE LIVES IN A FOURTH-FLOOR APARTMENT in a building in Trastevere. The neighbourhood is a tangle of wet alleyways, tall, dark tenements, and small, noisy bars. The narrow streets trap the damp from the river and the rain from the sky. It is always humid in Trastevere. The walls echo with Vespas, and the smell of exhaust fumes fills the streets. The narrow bars stink of cigarette smoke, coffee grounds, cheap wine, and—in winter—damp wool. Night comes early in Trastevere, and the light dies quickly, in the huddled, narrow streets under the steep western hill. If you look up, you can see a statue of Garibaldi, the Liberator, silhouetted against the sky.

Tonight she is giving a party.

"Let's see." She is dressed in oversized canary-yellow pants—room for two more people—with giant scarlet-and-white polka-dot suspenders, which she holds out or snaps for emphasis. She runs the tip of her tongue over her lips. "I'm going to prepare something special, something scrumptious." She begins to sort out what is in the kitchen. "Let's see: almonds, avocados, lentils, string beans, oranges, lemons, red peppers, Indian corn, onions, the leftover lamb and...It'll take absolutely hours to do. Think of all the hours in the warm kitchen! How delightful!"

Each week she makes a hugely complicated goulash, pouring in spices, herbs, meats, sauces, and anything else she can lay her hands on. Then they eat it for days, soaking bread in it, spooning it out between gulps of red wine. While she works, he sits at the kitchen table in his black jeans and black T-shirt and reads her snippets from the newspaper—"Bride Chops Off Groom's Penis"—until ordered to chop onions or slice tomatoes or run down to the corner grocer's for hot peppers or peanut butter.

She stirs the goulash, ladles out a spoonful and holds it out to him.

He leans forward, burns his lips, tastes the goulash. "Mmm." He nods. "Gosh, that's good!"

She holds the spoon to her mouth and blows. "Oh! Oh, yes, you speak the truth, dear sir. This is really good! Scrumptious!"

"Bridegroom Uses Ice Cubes to Arouse Bride."

"Really! Not very original, I'm sure. You'd think these chaps could think up something new. The clitoral orgasm, the G-spot, earlobe-tickle orgasm, the tit-clip orgasm, the stiletto, the latex or spandex orgasm, the dildo, the vibrator orgasm, the ice-cube orgasm, I say, there are lots of orgasms...when you think about it. Here, chop up these."

"Onions? I'll cry."

"No you won't."

"I will."

"Oh, please don't cry!" With onion-scented hands she

takes his face and kisses him lightly on the lips. Together, their lips taste of sweet goulash.

He wants to say, "I love you."

He almost says it. He almost says, "I love you." It is on the tip of his tongue.

Do I dare, he thinks, do I dare...?

Eat a peach, he thinks, thinking of his bald spot, of his paunch, of his liver, of being suddenly breathless climbing up the stairs.

The goulash is steaming on the table and the candles flicker. Most of the guests are innocuous. A black American girl stands by the window for a long time and talks to him about the Gulf War, which is about to begin. She has long, fine-boned hands, which he notices, and which she uses in the Italian way, gesturing, laying her long fingers on his arm for emphasis. Her English, too, has taken on an Italian inflection and grace.

There are punk artists and models in chalk-white make-up. They are young and innocently playing at depravity. Or perhaps they are not so innocent after all. What, after all, does he know about who or what they are? There is a famous photographer with a shaved head, chains, and tight black leather trousers. Some of the women have rings piercing their nostrils and wear purple lipstick. The men, mostly, have tight black stubble and nocturnal complexions.

Tell me, tell me all about yourself.

Yes, really, I really want to know.

How can you love unless you know all there is to know?

That's interesting, that's an interesting point. I never thought of that.

How can you be loved, truly, unless you are known, entirely, all of you? Even your most secret self. Secret selves.

Secret selves?

Yes, secret selves. I am a multitude, the poet said.

Yes, I like that. That is interesting. It was Walt Whitman, wasn't it?

Yes.

Kneel down. Submit! Say "bow wow."

"Bow wow!"

"Woof! Woof!"

Somewhere someone is exploding fireworks. The boom, boom, boom echoes against the studio's windows.

It is almost Christmas. The wall of glass has frosted up, crystalline. The black girl turns again to the window, spreads her hand against the cold glass.

"Can't see anything," she says.

Booom!

Boooom!

"No. Can't see anything," she says. But he can see her, her face in profile. Yes, he thinks, she is a Nubian goddess.

"Goodbye, goodbye!" The girls dressed in black disappear to their flat next door. The black American girl left early with her Italian husband. Finally the last leather jacket ambles off into the night.

They wash the dishes. She yawns and stretches. She is wearing long red underwear with a flap at the backside, cartoon long johns.

Outside it is deadly cold.

In the kitchen a paper is lying on the table, and he glances at the headlines. "Devil Changes Woman into Werewolf. Shocking photos on page 16."

"What I always wanted to be." She stretches and yawns.

"What?" He is carefully towelling the inside of a glass.

"A werewolf."

"You?"

"I have my dark side too."

"You do?"

"Yes. I do. I really do. You think I'm bovine and placid, dormant as a swamp. But I'm not." She yawns again, takes the last wineglass from him and places it upside down on a shelf. "Enough."

She turns out the light. They stand in the dark for a moment, then walk down the corridor to the bedroom. Silhouetted, she looks like a shaggy ballerina.

The big window is still frosty with cold. Ice is growing on the inside. The candles flicker on the table. Hopping on one foot, he pulls off his shoes, steps out of his trousers, throws his black T-shirt and underpants at a vague chair. Beyond the chair and the window, there is no moon, just the misty glow of the city.

Then they crawl between the clammy sheets. They

shiver. They cling to each other. Slowly they move their hands on each other's skin.

"Hold my feet," she says. "Yes, yes, yes—like that, just like that.

"You are very warm," she says, "so warm."

"You are warm too," he says, "so warm."

"But not my feet."

"No, not your feet."

She was English. He was Canadian. She was twenty-three. He was fifty-six. She was a computer graphics artist and kept a small Macintosh in one corner of her bedroom. Four times a week, she worked as an artist's model for the Academia. "Hours lying around naked and bored and getting stiff in your joints in a drafty room in front of a lot of people you don't know," she said, "then you get to know them, and, if the pose is not impossible, you can observe them observing you." In her spare time, she read books of philosophy—Plato, Hegel, Aristotle, and Wittgenstein.

He was a diplomat and economist and spent his days in meetings, drinking coffee and drafting memoranda, and, sometimes, inspecting disaster spots around the globe, flying low in a helicopter over endless refugee camps. "You look down through this bubble of glass and see them, all those bodies, gleaming in the sun, or dull with dust, shrunk with starvation and age, and you know they are dying, and there is nothing that can be done about it, not soon enough anyway. And you think how easy it would be to be one of them—you could be looking up at that helicopter flying over, from another world, and you'd feel the dust, the thirst, the hunger, the hopelessness of it—the lassitude."

"It's not always easy to be a person," she says. "A human being, I mean."

"No."

"I don't think I'll ever grow up." She stretches—twining her wrists above her head in mock bondage—a god, a goddess.

"I haven't."

"No, and I don't think, my dear sir, that you ever will." She puts her arm over his shoulder and leans her cheek against his. "My child, my love," she says.

He has to remind himself that she is twenty-three and he is fifty-six.

Together, just the two of them, they celebrate Christmas Eve. They eat too much and they drink too much. They go to sleep immediately—a water pipe is broken, the heat has been cut off, and it is icy cold in the apartment.

Early on Christmas morning, bundled up against the cold, they go to a café she frequents. She seems to be loved everywhere she goes—like a local star or a celebrity. The owner opens his arms, kisses her, pumps her hand, and shouts to everyone—"*Vedete chi c'è!* Look who's here!" They get free coffee, chocolate, and croissants.

A fat old man comes in. His fly is unzipped and his shirt is hanging out underneath his tweed jacket, which is hanging askew. His hair is long and white and wild and dirty. He is drunk. He greets her, he embraces her, he kisses her.

"He's a poet," she explains, "a local poet."

"Oh."

"He writes in dialect, Roman dialect."

"Oh."

The poet takes his brandy from the bar and turns to her and starts to explain something very long and complicated in a slurred, urgent voice. She leans forward, bending her head to catch every word.

Watching her with the poet, he realizes he is jealous, he realizes he has presumed too much, he realizes that she has a life—that she has a dozen lives—beyond his. He realizes that he needs her and wants her. How can she be so undiscriminating, he thinks, as to be friends with that old fart?

He suddenly realizes that in the drunken old poet he sees a parody of himself. This, he thinks, is you.

Yes, that's what you are, old and desperate, and desperately clinging.

A few days later, out walking alone, he suddenly feels tired and so he wanders to a city monastery and sits on a bench and listens to the fountain. The water drips slowly. The flowers in the courtyard are still in bloom, and the sun is warm on the leaves and on the burnt-sienna walls.

He turns his face up to the sun, closes his eyes and listens, just listens—to the water flowing, to a bird twittering, to someone's feet crunching on the gravel pathway, to the gentle rustling of a breeze, high above, in the fronds of a palm. He opens his eyes. The sky is still bright, still pitiless, and the air has darkened, the chill intimation of a winter night.

He stands up and wanders into the church. The air is damp and glows gently with incense and the warm odour of candles. He sits on a wooden bench, towards the back of the church. A white-haired priest is offering communion to two old ladies. There is also a young woman in a black suit— black jacket, short black skirt, black stockings and high heels. She is wearing a hat, and a dark veil. She stands up, goes forward, and kneels, her head bent, to take communion.

Above the altar is the Christ, gaunt and bloody, his eyes imploring heaven.

Drink this wine, for it is my blood...

Take this bread, for it is my flesh...

Bevete del vino.

Drink this, he thinks as he goes out into the bright day, the blue sky already darkening. Drink this: it is so primitive. You eat the flesh of a body to become that body. You devour a body to take on, in your own flesh, the gift of love of that body; to take on the attributes—the charity, the love, the passion, the strength—of that body, of that person, of that god. You drink the blood in order to be saved. Over the altar the Christ crucified had dripped blood, his eyes turned in anguish to the heavens, to the church's vaulted ceiling— earning pardon, in his suffering and death, for all of the sins of mankind.

Clutching his coat collar and looking up at the darkening sky, he thinks: no, in the end, we humans have to forgive each other—without forgiveness the chain of revenge and hatred would go on forever.

By drinking the wine, by drinking the blood, you are forgiven.

He was not a believer. Strictly speaking, he was an agnostic, though in practice, he supposed, he was an atheist, a mystical atheist, entranced by *maya*—imprisoned, with a certain amount of unease, in that veil of glittering illusion, that manifold of buzzing phenomena which is the world.

Drink this, my blood, he thinks, drink this, my blood. It is such a primitive and powerful idea. He sees naked warriors painted in clay, drinking the blood of the leopard. He sees hunters, half-human, on the steppe or in the jungle, draped in the skin of the beast. He sees a serial killer, in an old farmhouse in Minnesota, gabbling incantations as, with thick, clumsy fingers, he gnaws on a tibia and clothes himself in the skin and hair of the woman he has just killed.

As he walks away from the church he wonders about the woman in black. He wonders whether she is a widow in mourning, an adulteress keeping her options open, a sinner in repentance, an aristocratic Roman paying formal tribute to family tradition, or just a devout young woman who always dresses in black when she goes to church.

They are in bed again. The heat has been turned on, but it will take time to warm up the big room. The ice drips from the windowpanes. Tapping her teeth with the cap of a black transparent Bic, she is reading a book, making notes. The tip of her tongue runs thoughtfully along her lip, pressed against the Bic.

He is making notes on a report: "The Impact of European Community Agricultural Price Support Policies on East African Agricultural Production." Mostly, though, he is watching her. In profile she frowns, thoughtful.

She places her hand on his belly. Lazily, she curls and uncurls her fingers.

She turns, looks, and shields her eyes. "That sky is acting up again," she says. The clouds above the dark western hill are incendiary, like a bright flamingo shoal of islands. The fluttery clouds are streaked, rippled, stippled with wispy blocks of charcoal black, and it all presses up, brilliant and multifarious and cold, against the lead-framed squares of the dirt-streaked window.

"Oh!" She yawns, abandons the book and the Bic and slides down into the bed, under the covers. He follows her. "I'm hung over," she says, her face close to his. "Me too," he says. "I'm randy—horny I think you say—when I'm hung over," she says. "Me too," he says. They make love, slowly, in a tender, desultory way, trusting and lazy, as if there was all the time in the world. Then they lie against each other, doing little, thinking, breathing, and talking, and finally drifting apart into the separateness of sleep.

After the first few weeks they make love rarely. It is too comfortable, he thinks. She is too good, I trust her too much, I like her too much. There is no edge, no hatred. In a way he is in awe of her, but it is a moral and aesthetic awe, not sexual, not animal. Not animal at all.

I'm becoming impotent, he thinks.

She is young, he thinks, she needs a young lover, that's what she needs.

A few days after Christmas, they get dressed and go out and drink a dark raw red wine that gives heartburn in a small bar where she knows the barmaid.

She tells him of past lives, of a long period when she was very young — seventeen — and lived with an artist. "We are still friends," she explains, "I adore him. I think, in so many ways, I'm still in love with him."

She and the artist lived in a one-room flat near a pub, she tells him, a pub where "everything was happening" in a middling city in England. Yes, everything was happening, right there, in that pub, that's what she felt.

"They all came back — all our friends — to the flat for drinks. You know those long, lazy Sunday afternoons. The Sunday newspapers spread all over the floor. The sun used to stream in the big window. It was so golden and warm. We had a Persian carpet. We had so many plants. Oh, so many plants! It was like a steamy jungle."

In his mind's eye, he sees it: the plants, the sun-warmed Persian carpet, the beer and the warm smell of the newsprint, the mild white light of England streaming down through the windows.

Each decade has its own smell, its own taste. It's a thought that often occurs to him — the taste of time.

He wonders at the indelible mark a first love usually leaves on a woman. There will always be a warm spot in her heart for him, the other man, her first lover. "Mine," the first lover thinks, as an artist might think of his creation, "mine, forever mine."

On New Year's Eve, at midnight, fireworks would go off all over the city.

They climb a long stone staircase to a promontory over-looking the city. At the top there are large monuments tilted here and there, a fountain, palm trees and umbrella pines and a balustrade. Young men in tuxedos lean against the balustrade, bright smiles in their dark handsome faces. An icy chill is in the midnight air, a definite crystalline chill. People's breaths make bright white clouds.

People are drinking cheap champagne or Prosecco from transparent plastic cups. It tastes raw in the wintry night air.

BOOM!

Thunder out of a winter sky. Roman candles — a spray of giant tears.

A nervous, thin girl, teeth chattering, is handing out drinks. Her light raincoat is slung over her shoulders, and she wears a tight formal gown, burgundy and strapless. It is as if she were almost naked; there are goosebumps on her bare arms. She walks awkwardly in her high heels.

"*Volete del vino? Questo Prosecco è buono. Veramente. Molto buono.*" She has a thin, vulnerable, child-like voice.

"*Grazie, grazie, grazie.*" People gather round, cups offered, accepting the wine. She is an improvised hostess, among strangers. She has good legs—thin, well-bred upper-class Italian legs.

"*Grazie, grazie.*"

BOOM!

"Look," he says. A spray of gold rises high in the sky.

BOOM!

BOOM!

"I've taken a lover." She's holding her glass in front of her, near her lips, looking at him across the glass. "I'm sorry."

"A lover?"

"He's very fine. As a lover, I mean."

"I see."

"He makes love like, well...He's very enthusiastic, really."

"I see."

"He's very good in bed."

"I see."

"Do you mind? Do you mind awfully?"

"Well..."

"I'm awful. I really am. I'm so sorry..."

"That's all right, I...I don't know what..."

"I didn't mean to blurt it out like this. I wanted to...I don't know what I wanted to do...I'm a klutz, really, aren't I?"

"Don't worry, don't worry, please."

The lights explode. BOOM! The Italian girl comes over. "*Bevete*," she says in her high, childish voice, "*bevete del vino*."

"Can you ever forgive me?"

"There's nothing to forgive."

"Please forgive me." There are tears in her eyes, catching the exploding light.

"I'm the one who needs forgiveness." He turns away; he can't look at her tears.

"*Bevete. Questo Prosecco è buono. Veramente!*" The girl pours more Prosecco into their glasses. "*Felice anno nuovo!*"

"*Grazie, grazie,*" they say, both of them, together. They touch glasses.

BOOM!

BOOM!

Then they stand apart, looking away. She turns to him, the flowering distant light catches the wet in her eyes, a shower of scarlet sparks, over the white, the iris, the pupil, along her skin, in her short coppery gold hair.

He looks at her eyes, her wet blind eyes. She raises her glass. He moves to her and they click glasses. He takes her in his arms.

"You're so good. Such a good man," she says.

"I know." He smiles. It is a sickly smile, he thinks, but at least it is a smile.

BOOM!

"From the first moment I saw you, I knew—how good you would be."

"I know."

"You are so good."

"I know. I know how good I am." He laughs. "You are very good too. Much better than I."

"Happy New Year." She touches his cheek with her lips.

"Happy New Year."

BOOM!

BOOM!

Sparks and a shower of gold.

"*Bevete, bevete del vino!*" The girl is aware something is amiss; she comes back, pours them more wine, looks into their eyes. She is so thin, she is shivering in her ball gown, her thin raincoat. "*Bevete, bevete del vino!*"

"*Grazie.*"

"*Grazie.*"

"Time to go home?" she says.

"Time to go home, darling." It is, he thinks, the first time he has dared call her darling—only now that she is lost to him does he dare.

A few days later, he met her new lover. He was Italian, tanned, high coloured, and with curly thick black hair. He looks like a Welshman, he thought. Trust her to fall for an Italian who looks like a Welshman. They went to lunch, the three of them, and drank too much wine. The Italian who looked like a Welshman was a nice man, eager, ingratiating, and—the thought occurred to him—unable to believe his good luck: a goddess, a Greek goddess. Yes, the Welsh Italian was startled at his good luck.

The Welshman lasted a month or two. Then she decided to move back to England.

He helped her pack. They didn't talk much, but he felt the old thrill and the old comfort, just being close to her, just helping her, just watching the way she turned to him and smiled, shyly now, slightly abashed now, newly a stranger now.

And then he drove her to the airport. She was dressed — it was unlike her — very fashionably, all in black, with a long black raincoat open on her charcoal business suit. The headlights caught the copper of her hair, short as always. "A profile to die for," his friend Laura had told him, before, long before.

In her black high heels she was as tall as he, perhaps a bit taller.

He kissed her, and she kissed him. It was very chaste. Then she turned away and walked quickly through passport control. He stood watching.

When she was on the other side of the glass, she looked back. He saw that her eyes and her cheeks were wet. She waved, smiled, turned her back, and walked swiftly away.

It was years later, when he returned to the city on business, that he found time to make a pilgrimage. He went to the same old church where he had watched the priest give communion to the old women and to the one young woman dressed all in black. But the church was empty and even the smell of incense was cold.

He sat down. The flayed Christ still hung on its cross, but it was merely a Christ and cross of wood and paint, splashes of scarlet for stigmata, white and blue paint for eyes, painted ovals straining for the ceiling.

No, for an instant it was not merely the Christ carved in wood. It was the flesh laid bare: skinless, exposed to the level of raw bone, the rib cage, the pelvis, the knobby knees. It was the knowledge of the impossibility of love; that's what it was.

The Road Out
of Town

FOUR HOURS BETWEEN FLIGHTS. Not much time.

"The past is another country." Who said that?

At the airport, I rented a car.

The village stood at the end of a narrow plateau covered in wide fields, bright farmhouses, and big barns with tall silos. The plateau rode like a saddle between two steep valleys, and at the bottom of each wandered a narrow, shaded stream. White fluffy clouds always stood, neat cumuli, stationary but adrift, over the peaked roofs of the clapboard houses and over the thick leafy trees of the village. Like puffs of white cotton fluff those clouds were stacked up in the deep blue that reached down and touched the trees.

Such are memories—like primitive paintings. *Naïf* is the word, I believe. Everything has the mysteriously uncouth and clumsy beauty of a child's first drawing.

Such memories hide more than they reveal. Like ancient snapshots, they have no depth, no meaning. Three nameless relatives caught in muddy sepia, blinded by a long-gone invisible sun. They are standing in front of a bush, their features obliterated by light.

It was on the road going into town that I suddenly remembered. It was not really a memory—more the flicker of an eyelid—a feeling of emptiness, an underlying darkness. I knew, with an instant certainty, that some part of the landscape, some part of me, was missing.

I pull the rented car over onto the shoulder and stop. I get out and feel the crunch of gravel under my feet, the glare of the raw country air in my eyes. I take a deep breath, blink the tears away, pull out a handkerchief and blow my nose. It's been a long time since I've been here, on this road, a long time.

Such a return makes you think that time has gone by too quickly; you suddenly wonder if you have had time to live at all. You wonder if your own life really existed. But it was a real life, all right, a life as real, and as evanescent, as today.

So you return. In an airport on an impulse you rent a car and you return.

Take that road out of town. Now, like I said, I was driving into town, and have stopped, like I said, on the rough gravel on the side of the road into town—but I always thought of it as the road *out* of town. *Out*—that was the word. Town was the place we were all going to leave, sooner or later.

Town? Well, now that I think of it, town's a big word for that small cluster of houses and trees. In truth, it was more a village; even the word *village* seems a pretence. Thirty houses or so, clustered together on a wedge of clay and moraine, gravel and sand, left by the glaciers. There were a hundred

people, maybe, maybe a hundred and fifty. And kids. Lots of
kids. People had lots of kids in those days and they had them
young. It was after the war, the forties and fifties, life was
abundant, exotic, hopeful, and the women wore light cotton
dresses with flowered designs and, yes, the kids were bright
like flapping splashes of coloured cloth. Like washing on a
line—fluttering, flickering.

I remember my first day at school. A tall wooden clapboard schoolhouse painted rust-red with white trim. I
looked through the fence and held on to the bars. Kids! All
those kids! Running. Shouting. And those high-pitched
squeals! Girls! Paradise it was, and I was terrified.

Being brought up a mile or so from town, on a farm, I
guess I was used to silence, to rare and muted colours, to
big open spaces, with the clouds drifting.

Thirty years or more.

Thirty years. Or more.

I shield my eyes and blink them open. I get back into the
Japanese car. I start the engine. As I drive into town I again
half close my eyes against the springtime glare. I try to
think; I try to remember.

On Main Street I stop at a Greek restaurant for a coffee. It has bright white-and-blue awnings. Inside it has
Greek music, white-and-blue curtains, pictures of the
Acropolis, a signed photo of Melina Mercouri. I sit in a window seat and look out at Main Street.

Main Street...

The houses have all become small shops. Brightly

coloured, with hand-painted signs, they have neat displays in all the front windows. I see a jeweller's workshop, a health food store, and there's a New Age place that advertises mystic stones, crystals, and dream-catchers. I've seen those dream-catchers and held them in my hands. They are fragile — like cobweb tambourines. They catch your nightmares while you sleep. Leave nothing but the good thoughts, or so they say.

The new sidewalks are broad, bare, pure white, poured concrete. They bounce the sunlight back into your eyes in a blinding glare. It is all new. In such a place, I think, there is nowhere to hide. But maybe, here and now, nobody wants to hide, not any more. There are no desires today that can't be flaunted and boasted of in the open air. I think of how we played hide-and-seek and how everything — houses, basements, autumn woods, barn lofts — was, once upon a time, so mysterious: doors opening onto infinity.

The people I see walking up and down, I don't know any of them. They wear holiday clothes. It's their village now. Tourists who come out on weekends to see a real old-fashioned nineteenth-century country village, preserved intact, improved even, and hygienic. A fresh coat of paint is applied every season, there's real espresso to drink, three restaurants, and real live artists sit all day in their studios doing what artists do. You can look at them and talk to them, if you're so inclined.

I sip the thick, sweet Mediterranean coffee. I think about the road out of town. Thirty years ago. Thirty-five, maybe. Maybe more. I feel myself frowning. Could it be forty? Forty years? I remember it, of course, that road. It was so narrow it barely had space for two cars. It had a high-pitched crown and the deep ditches on both sides were overgrown with long grass. The asphalt was coarse-grained, pebbled, grey, brown, and black; it was patterned, if you stared long enough, like innumerable galaxies.

The oak trees that lined the road cast deep shadows. Those trees had been there a century or more, I guess.

Could it really be forty years?

In spite of the air-conditioning I wipe my brow and feel my heart sink and I quickly order another cup of thick Mediterranean coffee.

In the shimmering summer heat, in those days, we would walk quickly from cool shadow to sweaty glare and back again to shadow. Under the oak trees you could feel the breeze against your skin. Craning your neck you looked up at clouds drifting through the high troubled crowns of the trees and saw that the earth and the trees were adrift, not the clouds.

Those trees were cut down an age ago. No sign remains they ever existed or cast thick shadows or sweetened and freshened the evening. The road has been widened, the ditches broadened and flattened, and the grass has been cut stubble-short; it lies dried out, crisp, and straw brown under the pale sun. The asphalt is a dark black industrial asphalt, smooth, gently cambered, and the right-of-way has been expanded, pushing back the fields, shrinking the horizon. All this is so you can move faster and smoother from place to place, all your windows rolled up, the air-conditioning on, not noticing you've been anywhere or anyplace for any time at all.

It's smaller than I remember it. All of it is foreshortened and bare, as if the past had shrunk. Shrunk? Maybe it is the present that has shrunk, withered, and died. Maybe the present has left the past just as it was—splendid in isolation, immortal, innocent as a picture—drunk with unknowing happiness, drunk with summer smells, and, in the long evenings, drunk with the amber and gold fluttering of leaves.

The Greek girl brings me the second coffee. She is very young. She looks thirteen. Maybe she's sixteen. Maybe she's eleven. She has sleek black hair tied back with a red ribbon, a bright, fresh smile, wonderful skin, and dark, lustrous eyes that catch for an instant the outside brightness, making her blind. I have seen her in Athens and Cairo, in Palermo and Tripoli, and on the streets of Marseilles. I try out a few Greek phrases. Delighted, she replies. She smiles. For her too, perhaps, home is far away. Postcards of Greek islands are pinned up behind the bar.

On the street outside a tourist bus passes.

A family disembarks from a dusty station wagon. The father wears a baseball cap at a high angle and dark wrap-around glasses. His face is tilted upward as if he were sniffing the air, staring down the sun.

The breeze drifts the white curtains inward. Brittle

spring light shifts on the table. It makes patterns on the coffee, and on my sun-speckled hands.

I sip the coffee and look at the shifting pattern of light on my hand.

Unbidden, memories come back.

One girl at school had a pale face and quick blue eyes sometimes so shifty and nervous they seemed like bright minnows trapped in two fishbowls.

But when she looked at you, she really looked at you.

Now I remember ... Skinny too, she was.

In summer her paleness vanished; she became a soft burnished nut brown. And the eyes became deeper, calmer, like two ponds. Outstare anybody, she could ...

Your eyes follow her with interest down the road. It's just before dusk, one of those warm, golden-red early evenings: the heat of the sun lies on the skin even when you move into the shade.

She was wearing shorts, the police report said later, she was wearing clean, freshly pressed khaki shorts, a white cotton T-shirt, white ankle socks, and old-fashioned, flat-soled canvas running shoes.

She walks out of town.

Catching the light of the sinking sun, the oak trees are highly coloured. They offer shade, hiding places, refuges. Under those trees—towards dusk—the air is feathery rich, strangely perfumed, full of hope. It's a time of life, just then, under the trees, a time of year, a time of day, just before dusk, when you never want to go to bed; a time when you know you will live forever.

She sits down for a minute in the shade of one of the trees, though it's hardly shade at this hour, just a shadowy coolness. Her back is against the rough bark and she can feel it through the thin cotton of her T-shirt.

She rubs her back against the bark.

It feels good, getting at that itch between the shoulder blades. It's an itch she's invented, just now, so she can scratch it. Such is happiness.

She's still fuming mad. Right now she's deciding whether to go back, shame-faced, to the house, to her old man, or to strike out on her own, somewhere, anywhere. Or maybe she could cut across the fields and hide somewhere close, lay low beyond nightfall, just to put the fear of God in him.

That'll make him sorry, she thinks, just maybe, that'll make him sorry, just maybe, that's what she thinks.

But then she stands up. She moves out and stands on the shoulder of the road.

At some point maybe she will stick out her thumb.

Doubtful, she stretches, yawning. She has a way of reaching around and scratching the back of her neck, high or low on the nape, near the delicate sculpture of vertebrae, the fine gold down glinting on honey skin. Doing this, she sticks out a skinny sun-burnished elbow. It's an awkward, boyish gesture. You have watched it often, this stretching, this twisting, this fragile awkwardness, and you feel—even now—

a subtle unease you shall never completely understand.

The heat paints a mustache glow on her upper lip. She makes an absent-minded backhanded wipe at it and it's gone. The back of her hand smells of clean salt and sun. She takes a good sniff, and then a deep breath of the clear drifting air of the open fields and ancient trees. Summer! For a moment, all anger forgotten, her heart is light, adrift, and happy.

Out she walks onto the edge of the narrow road, loose gravel steeply sloping away.

Does she stick out her thumb?

Maybe.

Or — seeing her — does the vehicle just stop? Is it perhaps a truck, or a pick-up, or maybe a car, maybe a travelling salesman, a soldier on leave, or maybe an old jalopy, a bunch of guys, drinking beer in the late summer afternoon, out on a joyride?

Or was it perhaps someone she knew? Someone she knew who said, "Hi, whatcha doin' all alone out here, young lady?"

"I'm damned mad out here, that's what I'm doin'," she would have said, because she liked to use bad words and had an unstoppable penchant for speaking her very own mind. In those days all strong words were bad words. And to speak one's own mind, when one was a kid, well... Times and people change. Given time too, she might have become an eccentric, a scholar, a lover, or a true lady.

And she climbed into the car, or up into the truck. To sit next to someone she knew.

But no — I prefer to think it was a stranger. I prefer to

think it was not a face I'd ever seen, nor she—not before that last day.

I prefer to think he took her far, far away. Perhaps he took her to a new life. Who knows?

But in truth her bones must lie somewhere close, undiscovered and totally forgotten, in unconsecrated ground.

I wonder how long even bones last in this rain-soaked, frost-bitten earth. It's a thought that comes to you when the dirt is iron-hard with ice, or when it is fresh, raw, laid open in the fields, filled with water, turned up, freshly ploughed, and the spring thaw reflects a pale and chilly sky.

Like I said, on the way into town I had stopped for a moment and shaded my eyes. Off in the fields is a new subdivision—a stand of big, ugly, false-brick houses, half-built, box-like and pretentious. Close together they stand in fields of churned-up mud. I can see the tufts of dead grass, the exposed clay, the deep ruts and pools of muddy rainwater. Like a chill in my bones I feel the poverty of this shallow land, the generations of labour once needed for mere subsistence, and now buried and forgotten forever. This is a land of frostbite, not a land where memory grows.

Yes, it was then, coming into town, that I had the first intimations of loss.

So I got back into the car and headed into town, feeling the need for strong, warm caffeine. Now I sit nursing the sweet, thick coffee.

♦♦♦

Maybe in that last summer evening the ride was fun at first. She sat on the edge of the seat of the pick-up, or the car, and looked out the dusty windshield at the golden light of evening.

Everything is new when you set off on an adventure.

Adrenaline pumping, anger still churning in her narrow chest, nerves fluttering in her flat belly, she stares at the green cornfields, at the golden wheat, at the grey sagging cedar fences, at the bright white clapboard farmhouses. They all parade past, theatrically lit, at twilight, as if she had never seen them before.

Everything is new, and everything, unknowing, is for the last time.

The high-crowned, narrow country road means you can't stop steering, so the man concentrates, makes desultory conversation, just a word or two, or a question, now and then, here and there, keeping a watch on her from the corner of his eye.

I wonder what sort of a voice he had.

I wonder if he asked her about herself.

Was he curious? I wonder. Or did he just ask her questions the way a travelling salesman will ask questions, to keep her in a good mood, to keep her guard down, to make her smile? Did he like her smile? I wonder. That bright, surprised smile that seemed to carry all the newness and innocence of the world?

I wonder if he had smooth or callused hands, if his skin was tanned, or rough red, or office-white?

She was one for quick repartee. She always had a wise-crack ready.

If she had grown up she would have known how to scold kids, how to shame them into good behaviour. Or, maybe, if she'd taken another road, she would have known how to win a court case or write an editorial, or edit a book, though such things in those days were unusual aspirations for a girl, especially for a girl from such a small town, and such a family. If you could call one drunken violent man a family.

Still, she stood at the top of her class. One year behind me.

Mabel Dunlap, who lived in a small three-room white clapboard house on a corner of Main Street, had seen her leave her father's house. Mabel says she heard the angry bang of the screen door. It exploded into the evening quiet. It echoed. I guess that put Mabel on alert.

Miss Dunlap was what in those days was called a spinster, and she had a front window—neatly painted, wood-framed, with ripply, dimpled, pre-industrial glass— which was her lookout. Through the distorting panes she watched us all go up and down Main Street like rippling cartoons out of a hall of mirrors in the funhouse at the country fair. This was still in the days of radio, when seeing things and looking at neighbours was a treat and true entertainment.

Wearing those bobby socks, she was, said Miss Dunlap, she stomped off like hell's blazes, she did, said Miss Dunlap. Miss Dunlap saw or at least told things in comic-book terms—maybe an effect of that dimpled glass—and she wrote them up for the local paper, which was published in a town ten miles away but had a whole page dedicated just to us. Once, that page was topped up by a banner headline in big black ink: "Village Quiet on Thanksgiving!" I guess nobody'd been there to walk up and down and Mabel had looked all day from behind the dimpled glass in vain for somebody or something, but nothing appeared at all. Mabel was our chronicler; without her our existence wouldn't have been complete. Wrapped rain or shine in an ankle-length dark blue overcoat, she kept her hair invisible under a tightly wrapped white kerchief. Her rimless glasses unsuccessfully tried to hide a clear, handsome face with pale blue intelligent eyes. Mabel saw most of what went on, but for herself she kept to herself. She was somewhat of a mystery, to me at any rate. I always wondered what she wore under that overcoat. A woman alone, in those days, was an unusual thing. In any case, on the top of Mabel's porch the Union Jack always flew, dawn to dusk, a bit of flapping colour.

I see the girl now. Earlier that same summer.

She's standing on the grocery store steps in those cut-off skin-tight faded blue jeans she liked to wear. One thumb is hooked in a belt loop. A halter-top moulds her skinny shoulders and small breasts. Her skin is tanned, and her smooth shoulder blades are like angel's wings sketched out in soft brown butterscotch.

"Come on," she says, "let's go. Let's have a look."

I follow her between two houses, between two narrow gardens, and down the forest trail. Quickly it goes into the woods, then slopes, steep and slippery, suddenly downward, towards the valley, towards the river.

She talked to me I guess because she sensed I wouldn't laugh at her or gang up on her or try to hurt her.

"What is it?" I say.

"You'll see." She glances at me over her shoulder, a shy look.

Her legs were skinny and smooth and berry-brown and the bones and tendons were smooth yet so clear you felt you wanted to draw them or hold them in your hands. She was so perfect, like a drawing of a little girl. Funny, I only realized it then, walking behind her. Or now, once again, decades later, drinking Greek coffee, as I see us both walking single file — her in front, me behind — down that path between the trees. Only then, only now, do I realize how beautiful she was.

The mound is covered in pine needles, and she crouches there and points down to the river: fifty feet of straight clay cliff below us, the river runs, rippling, shallow, running over rocks, catching the sun.

Down there, in the mud flats next to the river, is the rusted-out carcass of a car. It looks to me like a Chevy, an old red Chevy with a crushed hood and roof. I'd read about it. And heard about it. She looks at it for a long time.

"That's where they died," she whispers.

I stare at the car.

"I wonder what it felt like," she says.

I look at her.

"To die," she says. Crouching there, her eyes narrow, looking at me as if it were a challenge — as if she expects me to object, to say something. Yet at the same time her eyes are far away, flattened by the light rippling up from the river, acquiring a curious animal simplicity, luminous, with no distinction between iris and pupil, just drifting ripples, crystals of light.

I look back down at the wreck and think about the flash flood, about the impact of a wave, the cold water, my fingers clamouring against the windows, scraping, fingernails breaking, grappling at the door, my fists banging silently, my eyes and nostrils and mouth and lungs filling with muddy, ice-cold water, thrashing blindly.

"Come on," she says. She reaches out to take my hand as if she were older than I, but we are almost the same age and I'm taller.

"Come on," she says. Her hand is smooth and dry and it is a shock to feel it in my hand.

"I want to try everything before I die," she says.

We stand next to the wreck. The black mud sucks at our bare feet.

"The kids don't like me because I'm different," she says. "And I don't know why I'm different." She looks at me as if it were a question. "I'm not different," she says.

I didn't know what made her different. She didn't have a mother, she only had a dad, that I knew, and she lived in a run-down, unpainted clapboard house on a corner of Main Street. "It's a shame, that house," said my mother.

There were petunias in a dirt flowerbed in front of the house and she was the one that put them there. I'd seen her, crouching early one morning, patting them down. Nobody was on the street. It was something secret she was doing. She hadn't seen me, and somehow I didn't want her to see me seeing her. So I slipped away.

I'd seen her dad on the sidewalk in town wearing his undershirt. His shoulders were white and hairy and he was tanned real dark and red at the neck and on his face. It looked funny and was weird. Nobody went outside in the village in their underwear. Her dad shouted sometimes too. Sometimes he had a bottle in his hand. I remember him shouting, "What the fuck you looking at, eh? What the fuck you looking at! Damned fucker!" It was a word you weren't supposed to use or even think. When I mentioned her name once, my mother just said, "Oh, that poor girl!" And then she wouldn't say any more. "There are certain things we don't talk about," my mother said, and she pretended to be busy, lifting up a book, leafing through a few pages and putting it back down.

"You're not different."

"Yes, I am." She reaches up and pulls some rust off the bent roof of the car. "Look!"

Rust flakes off, falls away. There was something religious about that overturned, rusting car, all alone, abandoned in the mud, water flowing around its broken tail lights and open trunk. It was like discovering a ruined temple, a place of secret sacrifice.

"I'm gonna do things," she says. She reaches up, chips off some more rust. "I'm gonna do things with my life. People just sit around. They think I'm like them. Just sitting around. I'm not like them." She chips angrily at the rust. It makes a long rusty trail on her arm from the wrist down to the elbow.

I'd never kissed a girl before.

I hardly even knew what kissing was.

I looked at the way she stretched up, at her legs, at the way the water reflected up on the tanned legs.

Two tendons stood out at the back of her knees, with the soft, cupped valley in between, like the smooth trace a finger would make.

"Come on," she says. She takes my hand again. Her hand is rough with a soft fur of rust.

We wade across the river. It is shallow, just water between white stones, pebbles, flat rocks, bubbling, gurgling, cool transparent water. Wouldn't harm a soul, river such as that, said my dad, a mere stream, so you wouldn't think, said my dad, you wouldn't think that it could so suddenly...

Her lips looked moist, bright, reflecting the water, which made circles jumping up and down on her face like a face in the midway mirrors.

I thought she wanted me to kiss her, so I put my lips against hers. It was the first time my lips had touched anybody else's lips. Hers were so soft. She looked at me, narrowed her eyes, and laughed.

♦ ♦ ♦

After that I didn't see her much. Our family went away to the cottage for the summer. When I came back she waved at me from her porch. I waved back, but I couldn't come over because I was with my dad in the car and because her dad was there and he didn't like her talking to people when he was around.

I thought about her. I thought about her a lot. I thought about her shoulder blades and her legs and her lips and the way she looked at me, narrowing her eyes, as if we shared something, some secret understanding, and as if she were just about to laugh.

A couple of times that summer, at the cottage, I mentioned her name. My mother said, "Oh, that poor child." That was all she would say, nothing more. Mentioning her name gave me a secret pleasure. We were secretly united, she and I, if I said her name. I imagined she might somehow know I was mentioning her name, that it would give her pleasure too, a secret pleasure.

"He must feel awful, poor man" is what somebody said, early that hot September. That was when I heard for the first time about how, furious with her dad, she'd walked out of the house, down Main Street—which was just two rows of houses on a narrow road with a broken sidewalk on one side, wrought-iron street lamps, a wooden-fronted store, and two crooked stop signs—down Main Street she walked, and out onto the road that led towards my place.

The road out of town.

Like I said, it was a real road then, with oak trees, and high-crowned, coarse-grained asphalt, and steep ditches overgrown with grass.

The fields came up close to the road, and you could hear the rustling of the wind, or of the breeze, in the oak trees, and the wind whispering through whatever was growing and leaning in close by, wheat, or hay, or corn, or just plain long grass. You could smell all the smells too, of the earth, and the trees, and the grass.

On the road out of town, coming to my house, first you went past the Lemieux homestead. It stood up on a little mound bright with a garden full of flowers and ivy on green latticework all around the porch. Then you passed the McFarlands' barn and farmhouse, big plain brick and wood buildings with lots of trees and an uncut lawn out front. Then you were on your own for a while—about half a mile—before you got to our house. It was a nice square brick house that my mother called Georgian because of the red bricks and false rustication and symmetry, I guess. She explained it to me once, but I've forgotten.

I would like the story to change, and I make up different endings.

I imagine that she comes to my house; she makes it to my house. That's where she'd always wanted to come, I imagine this to myself. And my mother calls up to me, "Your friend is here," and I go, and she looks at me, and she says, "I've run away from home, so I came here."

Or she doesn't say anything, but we invite her to supper and she sits at the table and...and she knows how to hold her knife and fork and says funny things that please my mother and father.

Or "I was thinking of you," she says.

Or, maybe she walks up the lane alone, beside the house, and she stands there, between the house and the apple orchard, in the golden light of the end of the day, and hollers my name out and...

But no, she just walked down the road.

Maybe she stuck out her thumb, maybe she didn't. Maybe she didn't get as far as my house. Maybe she got her ride before she got to my house, and then...

Funny, but in all these years I have not thought of her. Not once. Not one single time. I had forgotten the very fact of her existence.

Until I saw the oak trees were gone. Cut down every one, vanished as if they had never been.

Then I realized that we are all gone, every one of us who lived through that summer, forty years ago.

Yes, forty years.

I finish the bittersweet coffee. I glance at my watch. I have to take the rented car back to the airport and get my baggage out of the deposit and check in. It's been just four hours between flights.

A lifetime.

I stand up. I pay and I thank the little Greek girl and her father. The little girl gives me two postcards from the Greek islands. Her eyes are bright and dark. The man smiles; he has gold in one tooth.

The rental-car people are very efficient. It takes five minutes. I check in my suitcase and, before I know what has happened, I am in my non-smoking window seat and the plane is racing down the runway.

I stretch and smile: tomorrow morning in Paris I do not have to work. I can have a café au lait and croissant, perhaps at the Deux Magots, perhaps at the Café Flore. I will read the morning papers. I will phone Suzanne or Laura. Perhaps I can arrange lunch with Sonia. We shall drink a bottle of wine. I shall smoke a cigar. Together we shall do some shopping. Perhaps it will rain; we will run, laughing, as if I were much younger than I am, and shelter under the plane trees along the boulevard Saint-Germain.

Yes, the trees...

I cultivate the sort of romanticism that makes me feel at home in that other place that has never been my place — memories of Hemingway, Glassco, Fitzgerald, Joyce, Malraux, Sartre, Camus, Balzac, and Proust. Of other people's stories, I make up my own memories, my routines, my rituals, and my consolations. My nostalgia is second-hand; it belongs to lives I have never lived.

Yes, perhaps Sonia, witty, irrepressible Sonia.

I look out of the airplane window. Long, straight glittering lines — headlights — stretch to the horizon. All those country roads have become highways. Across the land crisscross immense geometric superhighways, toll roads, industrial parks, anonymous malls, and endless suburbs.

Cement and asphalt and brick cover the fields and the woods, the valleys and the streams, the memories and the hearts. The lights glitter in marching multitudes. The commuters are on the move. It is twilight time, the hour of migrations: "Home, I am coming home."

To the west, the sun flares out in one last gigantic blood-red fireball, out over the Great Lakes, over the Precambrian rocks and bogs and forests of the Canadian Shield, and over the immense flat prairies, and over the west, the mountains and the islands. This is the land. Over the West Coast, where it is still afternoon, the sun will still be shining. Here the sun, as it sets, sucks up great strata of dark angry dust from the immense city. Above, already, there is a deep blue, so deep, so pure it is almost like blindness, and a few stars shine.

"*Monsieur?*"

The stewardess leans down. I look up from my paper — more killing in Bosnia — and smile. Her blue eyes are very bright, Norman eyes, and the blond hair is Norman hair. She is very handsome, a daughter of Viking conquerors, a daughter of the fair fields of France, where the poppies grow. Her eyes reflect, in small ovals, the night sky, the translucent, transcendent blue, and a suggestion of stars. Her accent is Parisian.

"Yes," I say in French, "yes, I would love a coffee."

I look once again out the window — the landscape has been left behind — now it is only sky.

Empty sky.

And deepening night.

Author's Note

The stories in *So this is love* were written over several years in Italy, France, and Canada, and they reflect, in part, the experiences of an expatriate in Europe in the years immediately following the sexual revolution of the 1960s and 1970s. In a sense, the stories reflect, in an indirect and minor key, the failure of the utopian aspirations — both public and private — of those years. They also reflect, of course, the incredible humour and generosity of the friends with whom I shared many of the adventures and experiences of those decades.

I want to thank Anna Porter of Key Porter Books, whose generous support made possible the publication of this book. And, in particular, I want to thank Janie Yoon, my editor, whose enthusiasm, talent, and acute critical sense have often saved me from myself. Thanks, too, to Karen Mulhallen of *Descant* magazine, permissions editor Ann-Marie Metten, and to Jackie Park and Claudia Neri for their invaluable friendship and advice.

And, above all, my gratitude goes to Dianne Rinehart — for making it all possible.